E.J. RUSSELL

THE LADY UNDER THE LAKE

QUEST INVESTIGATIONS
BOOK THREE

The Lady Under the Lake
Copyright © 2022 by E.J. Russell

Cover art: L.C. Chase, http://lcchase.com
Edited by Meg DesCamp

ISBN: 978-1-947033-37-5

First edition
January 2022

Contact information:
ejr@ejrussell.com

E.J. RUSSELL

THE LADY UNDER THE LAKE

QUEST INVESTIGATIONS
BOOK THREE

Dedicated to my readers, who are determined for Matt to find his place, and with apologies to Raymond Chandler for hijacking his title without being anywhere close to noir.

CONTENTS

CHAPTER ONE

"Does Zeke know you're coffee-cheating on him?"

Eleri glared up at me from under her shiny brown bangs. "I'm not *coffee-cheating*. I'm engaging in *beverage diversification*." Her gaze shifted to the woman behind the cash register at Wonderful Mug Coffee Shop and her expression went—dare I say it? No, I couldn't, not out loud. Eleri might classify herself as my BFF, but she tended to take exception when anybody other than her broke out the dryad humor.

Oh, what the heck. I needed to vent a little steam somehow.

"If I didn't know you better," I murmured as we moved toward the counter, "I'd call that look positively...*sappy*."

She tore her gaze away from the cashier to glare at me again. "I will *hurt* you, Hugh."

I smirked down at her. "You won't. You *luuuurrrve* me. In a very platonic way, of course."

"You know," she said, eyes narrowing, "for somebody who's probably getting some regularly, you're in a remarkably prickly mood. I'd have thought Lachlan would have banged you into a state of bliss by now."

At her mention of my almost-boyfriend, it was my turn to scowl. "We haven't been able to follow up on that lead on Wyn's whereabouts yet." Was I whining? Yeah, probably. After our last case at Quest, a grateful Herne the Hunter had gifted us the location of Lachlan's soon-to-be-ex-husband, and I'd had visions of falling into bed with my selkie hottie before dinner. "We drove all the way to Eugene and then the beaver clan who owns the lake wouldn't let us launch Lachlan's new canoe. Apparently there was some coming of age thingy for one of their kits. No outsiders allowed. Then Lachlan got a last-minute fishing trip call." Followed by back-to-back bookings for the last two weeks, curse Oregon's unexpectedly sunny October weather.

Eleri gave me a wicked grin. "Guess those best *laid* plans went a little agley, eh?"

"Shut up, or I'll tell Zeke you've been scoring lattes behind his back." Our demon office manager kept us well supplied with some of the best coffee in the known universe, given his access to druid-blessed coffee beans.

She sniffed. "We're not *exclusive*. Besides"—her expression shifted to her usual lively mischief—"he's distracted this morning."

I blinked. "Wait. You've already been to the office? Why do you need Wonderful Mug then?"

She rolled her eyes. "Oh, please. You of all people should be able to sympathize with a little extracurricular flirting. Unresolved sexual tension for the win," she said when the cashier—Sierra—smiled brightly at her, before calling an older man over to the register and taking her place behind the espresso machine.

I frowned. "Sierra's a barista now?"

Eleri's cheeks turned pink beneath her tan. "Only for me."

I narrowed my eyes. "Exactly how often do you come here?"

"None of your business."

"She's *human*, Eleri."

"I could make the obvious response, Hugh, but that would be beneath us both."

I flinched, but tried to cover it with a cough. You know, sometimes I actually forgot? That *I* was human too? I was surrounded by the supernatural community at work *and* in my personal life, given that I was sort-of-dating a selkie. But my knowledge and participation were the exception. Most humans had no idea that supes walked among them.

Unless said supe screwed up and gave themselves away, thus endangering not only themselves, but their human friend-slash-paramour and the entire paranormal community.

I was learning there were exceptions, grandfathered in when the Secrecy Pact was initiated after virtually all the European-born vampires migrated to the United States through Faerie following World War I. Long story, but the only part of it I was interested in personally was the selkie-human relationship exception clause that meant Lachlan and I could actually be together once he severed the handfasting knot with his fae husband.

Something that would be a lot easier once we actually *found* the man.

Since I wasn't totally lacking in self-preservation instincts, I chose to ignore that particular conversational black hole. I cleared my throat. "Zeke's distracted, so you're doing him a favor by scoring contraband beverages?"

"Not contraband, Hugh. You're as bad as my clan chief," she groused, "blathering on about how we shouldn't drink anything but unfiltered rain water, same as our trees. *Tradition*." Her voice was loaded with disdain. "Bah. Nothing but an excuse for laziness if you ask me."

"I don't know," I said as we stepped up to the counter. "Some traditions are okay." I was depending on one in particular. Counting on it, in fact. But the selkie/human loophole was one that expanded freedoms. Eleri's clan chief seemed only interested in the traditions that removed them. I couldn't blame Eleri for trying to—yep, I was going there—*stick* it to him.

"Same again, Flora?" Sierra called, addressing Eleri by the Mug name I'd given her the first time I'd dragged her to the shop.

"*Again?*" I murmured. "You've been here already *today*?"

She elbowed me in the ribs and smiled at Sierra. "Absolutely. And a flat white for my annoying friend here. He could use the extra caffeine."

Sierra grinned at me. "Morning, Hugh. Nice to see you again."

"You too, Sierra," I said with a somewhat forced smile. After Eleri graciously allowed me to pay for both our drinks, I dragged her over near the windows while we waited for Sierra to prepare them. "Exactly how distracted *is* Zeke?"

"Very." Her peat-brown eyes sparkled, although I wasn't sure if it was because she dearly loved gossip—all fae did—or because Sierra kept casting her flirty glances over the milk steamer. "The *King* and *Queen* are coming to our office today."

I blinked at that. "The King and Queen. Of Faerie?"

She nodded. "Mmhmm. And Zeke's freaking out a little, trying to make sure everything is perfect."

"Why? Not why is Zeke dithering, but why are they coming to us?" Since Niall O'Tierney, one of our Quest bosses, was the King's half-brother, interacting with His Majesty wasn't completely unheard of, but most of the time *we* went to *him*. And as far as I knew, the Queen had never crossed our threshold. She never left Faerie. Maybe because she sort of *was* Faerie, or at least its avatar. I mean, I'm sure Niall must see both of them more often, although my brain stuttered at the image of what a Sunday dinner at their Keep must be like.

"I *think*," she said, low-voiced, "that Niall's getting ready to propose to Gareth. He's consulting with Their Majesties about the details."

"He doesn't need their permission, does he?" Niall's boyfriend, Gareth Kendrick, was the last true bard in Faerie, and in the past, their union might have been problematic, given that Niall was Unseelie fae and Gareth was Seelie—think Chaotic Neutral and Lawful Good. But after the Convergence that merged the two spheres, the fae were all one big dysfunctional family now. Besides, the King was Unseelie and the Queen was

Seelie, so any cross-sphere objection would be pretty hypocritical.

She chuckled. "Not permission. I think Niall's actually *nervous.*"

"Nervous? Are you serious? He and Gareth have been in love for literally two centuries. He can't be afraid Gareth's going to say no, is he?"

"Love is a funky thing, Hugh," she said, her gaze resting on Sierra. "It screws with your logic."

"Good point," I muttered. My own relationship wasn't exactly logical. All I can say is if you'd ever met Lachlan in all his upright, grumpy glory, you wouldn't question it in the least. "So are you just going to hang around here all day, sucking up more caffeine than is good for you and making goo-goo eyes at Sierra?"

"I do *not* make goo-goo eyes," she said, totally making goo-goo eyes. "I'm here to meet Blair."

"Blair?" I blinked. "Lachlan's friend Blair?"

She nodded. "It's some kind of teacher development day, so they don't have school. I like the kid, and since you're spiriting Lachlan away on another Wyn hunt, I volunteered to hang out with them." She wrinkled her nose. "The less time they have to spend around their revolting father, the better."

I liked Blair too. "You don't have to. They could come with Lachlan and me."

She huffed. "Please. Like I'd expose them to that. They're only twelve. You'd probably scar them for life."

I gaped at her. "We'd never do anything in front of a *kid*! We won't do anything, anyway. Once we find Wyn, he and Lachlan still have to go through the sundering ceremony before Lachlan's officially unmarried." Lachlan, stickler for keeping his promises that he was, refused to so much as kiss me on the mouth while he was still married. We'd had some world-class hugs—and there *might* have been a little friction involved, if you know what I mean—and he'd kissed my hand and the top of my head, but nothing more. And you know what? Eleri had a point about unresolved sexual tension. Because *yowzer*. The anticipation was approaching critical mass with every heated look Lachlan tossed me.

That didn't mean I wanted it to go on forever, though. Remember my boss and his two hundred year relationship? Yeah, supes are really long-lived. Humans? Not so much. I wasn't willing to wait until I was past my sell-by date to hook up with Lachlan.

But with any luck, today we'd remove our last big impediment and be that much closer to our own personal supernova.

Sierra bustled over to us wearing a purple pea coat that matched Wonderful Mug's signature to-go cups, two of said cups in her hands. "Here you go. I'm all set."

I took my cup, giving Eleri the side-eye as she took hers. "All set?"

Eleri lifted her chin. "Once Lachlan drops Blair off, we're going to the zoo," she said almost defiantly.

Sierra grinned, dark eyes crinkling at the corners as she retrieved two more cups from the counter. "Animals smashing pumpkins! It's the best. We're meeting my ex there, along with her sisters and niblings." Sierra must have read the shock on my face because she buffeted my arm. "We're still friends, Hugh. No drama at all."

"Right," I said doubtfully as Lachlan's truck pulled up outside. "Looks like my ride's here."

The three of us left the shop and clustered on the sidewalk in the chilly breeze. Lachlan got out and circled around the front of the truck, his hands in the pockets of his sea-green anorak. "Good morning, Matthew." I still shivered whenever Lachlan said my name—*MattHugh*—like he could see both sides of me: Matt Steinitz, ex-tabloid photographer, and Hugh Mann, Quest investigator. He nodded at the two women next to me.

"Ladies." He lifted his left eyebrow, the one with the scar bisecting it.

Since Sierra was gazing up at Lachlan, her eyes wide, I said, "Lachlan, this is Sierra Rose. Sierra, Lachlan Brodie."

"Wow." She held out a hand to shake his. "You look exactly like Jason Momoa as Aquaman."

Lachlan's lips quirked. "So I've been told." He opened the passenger door for Blair to climb out.

The kid seemed a little paler than when last I'd seen them, not that they'd ever looked especially robust in their oversized army surplus jacket. Their long brown hair whipped in the breeze, almost as though it had a life of its own, probably because Blair wasn't wearing their rainbow beanie. However, they were sporting a pair of narrow, rectangular glasses that I didn't remember from the other times we'd met, the red frames matching the sweater under their jacket—a sweater I knew Lachlan had purchased for them.

"Hey, Blair," Eleri said brightly. "Cool glasses!"

"Thanks," Blair murmured. As usual, they didn't focus on anyone's face—they had a condition called prosopagnosia, facial blindness. However, they had an excellent memory for other features—relative size, voice timbre, and fashion choices. Their smile dawned when they spotted Eleri's forest green Doc Martens.

"This is my friend, Sierra. We'll be meeting some of her friends at the zoo."

"I'm pleased to meet you, Blair." Sierra held out the second cup. "This is for you, if you like hot chocolate. If not, I can whip you up something else before we go."

"I like hot chocolate." They took the cup. "Thank you. Your coat's the same color."

Sierra grinned. "When something works, it works. Know what I'm saying?"

Lachlan rested one big hand on Blair's shoulder. "Call me if you need me. Otherwise, I'll pick you up this afternoon."

:

"Oh stop fussing, Lachlan," Eleri said, linking her elbow with Blair's. "We're going to have fun and won't think about you even once. Right, Blair?"

Blair smiled up at her with the same hero worship they reserved for Lachlan. "Well, maybe once."

Lachlan chuckled. "I'll not take that personally. Have a good time." He opened the door and gestured me inside with a smile that made my toes curl. "We've got an appointment to keep, Matthew, if you're ready."

I raised my cup in farewell to Eleri, Sierra, and Blair, and practically leaped into the truck—not easy, since it had no running boards and the cab was about three feet off the ground, but I managed. Heck, I practically flew.

Because the end of my very long, very dry spell was in sight at last.

CHAPTER TWO

I don't know if I've mentioned it before, but Lachlan Brodie can be a pretty grumpy cuss with a side order of uncommunicative. So in a way, I wasn't astonished that by the time we passed Salem on our way to Eugene and the beaver clan's lake, he hadn't said more than a dozen words to me.

However, he usually showed me a softer side of himself, something probably nobody other than Wyn had ever seen.

Well, Wyn and Blair.

Oh. Blair.

I studied his profile, his blade of a nose, the crest of his cheekbone, the hair waving onto his shoulders. His eyebrows were drawn down—from this angle I couldn't see that scar, dammit—and though his mouth was set in a firm line, he wasn't *technically* scowling. Trust me, when Lachlan scowls, you know it.

"Are you worried about Blair?" I asked softly.

"A bit." He glanced briefly at me with an apologetic smile. "I'm sorry I'm such poor company today, Matthew"—*shiver*— "but that bloody wanker of a father of theirs makes me want to spit. He told them yesterday that he'd changed his mind about letting Blair come along today because they'd broken their glasses."

I blinked. "But their glasses looked fine."

He glanced sidelong at me. "Their *old* glasses. That broke two weeks ago." He chuckled a little ruefully. "Granted, I think they broke them on purpose, but the prescription was so old, it wasn't doing any good." Lachlan's scowl returned. "I made the blighter—"

"Does this man have a name other than blighter or bloody wanker?" I asked mildly.

"He doesn't deserve one," he growled.

"Lachlan."

"Fine. It's Floyd."

"His last name wouldn't be Pink, would it?"

Lachlan's eyebrows bunched in confusion. "No. Sayer. Why?"

I sighed. Really. Supes and their lack of popular culture context. "Never mind. What did you make Floyd do?"

"Get Blair an eye exam."

"And let me guess. You bought the new pair." When Lachlan didn't respond, I knew I'd gotten it right. "I take it Blair was disappointed about Floyd's decision?"

Lachlan's lips quirked and he shook his head. "Well, the mite has a temper, which I confess I'm glad of. They're not downtrodden, although they're still wary of trusting the agencies that could protect them."

"Yeah," I said. My coffee had gone cold by around Woodburn, but I held onto the cup just for comfort. "Once you're in the system, it's a crap shoot about where you'll land or how you'll come out the other side. Especially for a nonbinary kid like Blair. Did they act out this time?"

Lachlan nodded. "Ate an entire bag of potato chips." He glanced at me again. "They've got a salt sensitivity, so they made themselves sick as a dog."

"Crap," I muttered. No wonder they looked pale this morning. "They're okay now, though, right?"

"Aye. Although they were miserable last night. I had to show up at Floyd's door to make sure he wouldn't use it as another excuse to keep Blair from the trip." The glance he shot me this time was a little shamefaced. "You don't mind that I brought them along? That I'll need to head back to the coast after we find Wyn? It'll take time to get the ceremony scheduled, so it's not as though we could be...well...together today."

My belly fluttered, but I forced a smile. "Of course not. Blair deserves some fun. I don't begrudge them that, nor their friendships with you and Eleri." I gazed out the window, not that the fields in Lane County were particularly interesting this time of year. As I did, I caught sight of the truck bed in the side-view mirror. The *empty* truck bed. "Where's the canoe?"

Lachlan chuckled. "The beaver clan doesn't want us on the water. It seems that their kits' first ever lodges aren't as sturdy as they might be, and they don't want to risk any damage."

"Then how—"

"Rusty Johnson and Casimir Moreau are letting us use their dock. The rest of the clan can't fuss about it because Rusty built the house on the opposite side of the lake from where most of them live—after Casimir bought all the other lots on that end of the lake." Lachlan chuckled. "Seems the two of them like their privacy." He winked. "Fond of naked midnight swims as they are."

I swallowed, my throat gone thick. "G-good to know." To distract myself from the image of Lachlan and *me* on a naked midnight swim, I looked everywhere but at him. That's when I noticed something else missing. "Where's your pack?"

Lachlan flicked on his turn signal and headed for the highway exit. "Back on my boat."

I turned in my seat, the better to frown at him. "But Wyn's at the bottom of that lake. How are you going to find him without your skin?" Before you ask, that's not as creepy a question as it sounds. Selkies are seal shifters, and they control their shifts by putting on or removing their seal skin, which resembles a very closely furred wetsuit more than a creepy eyeless seal that's been boned by a Ginsu knife.

"I couldn't swim in the lake anyway, lad, not in my skin." His smile glinted as the sun slanted in through his window. "Not my seal skin, anyway. Selkies are salt water folk. The lake's fresh water."

"So what would happen?" My eyes got round. "You *can* swim, can't you? I mean, without shifting? You wouldn't drown?"

"I can swim, and I wouldn't drown, but I couldn't shift either. It takes the touch of the sea to keep me in seal form."

I folded my arms. "Why does none of the selkie lore mention that?"

"Think back on all the selkie tales you've read or pestered me for. Have any of them taken place anywhere but by the sea?"

"Well. No."

He turned onto a road marked *Private*. "There you go then. Maybe we like to keep a few secrets to ourselves." He winked at me. "We're not like you humans, who want to share every little thing about our lives with the world, whether the world cares about it or not."

You humans. Yep, there's still a divide, but with Lachlan, it's always seemed like my humanity was more of a turn on than a drawback. Eleri had once told me, *"Selkies and humans. It's a thing."* Yeah, I was counting on that traditional *thing*. A lot.

"So if you can't dive into the lake and invite him topside for a little chat, how will we get his attention?"

Lachlan patted his anorak pocket. "Your friend Dr. MacLeod gave me a wee calling card."

I blinked. "Bryce?" My other boss, Mal Kendrick, was married to a druid. I narrowed my eyes. "It's not a potion, is it? Mal always says druid potions are nasty." Since Bryce was an environmental science professor as well as a druid, I knew better than to think whatever magical doodad he passed along would hurt the lake or its denizens. But that didn't mean it wouldn't hurt Lachlan, or at least cause him significant discomfort.

"Nay. Just a little message I'll float along on the water, to let Wyn know he's safe and we'd be grateful for a chat."

On the one hand, good that the *calling card* wasn't too invasive. On the other hand, I'd prefer to deliver a more forceful message to Wyn. Something along the lines of *Get your ass up here and divorce Lachlan already.*

Lachlan pulled the truck onto a gravel drive that snaked through the woods and ended at a beautiful, sprawling Craftsman-style house right on the lakeshore. While the shrubs along the flagstone walk leading to its wide front porch were neat and healthy—I suspected a dryad gardening service—they weren't particularly well-established. "This is new?"

He nodded. "Finished last spring. A wedding present from Rusty to Cas."

I frowned at him. "How do you know so much about them?" I'd met both men—Casimir was the youngest vampire in the country, and would remain so since one of the conditions for that mass vampire rescue/exodus was a moratorium on turning anybody else. Rusty was a beaver shifter, but Inactive—unable to shift—so he was effectively human, although it didn't seem to bother either him or Cas.

"The water-based supe community isn't that big. I've known Rusty for years. We're both…at odds with our clans, although for Rusty, it's them rejecting him. With me, it's the reverse. We've tipped a few pints in our day."

We got out of the truck and I looked around. The house's windows were all covered with blackout shades—which made sense, given that a vampire lived there. "They're not at home, are they?"

Lachlan shook his head. "Nay. They're at Cas's place in Portland this week. Some kind of benefit for the hospital." He gestured to a gravel path on one side of the house that led toward the lakeshore. "The dock's down that way."

We crunched down the slight slope toward the dock that extended fifteen feet or more into the lake. There was a small structure next to the dock, but it was completely on land, clearly not like the boathouses that dotted the far shore. "If they don't have any boats, what's that building for?"

Lachlan grinned at me. "Best not to ask, lad. But when they're done with their naked swims, maybe they'd prefer not walking all the way back to the house."

My jaw dropped. "You're kidding. It's a *wank* shack?"

He studied the building, head tilted. "More than a shack, I'm thinking. I'd reckon more than wanking too, but also not our business."

Lachlan took my hand and led me onto the dock, our footsteps echoing hollowly. When we got to the end, he sat down and patted the boards next to him. "Have a seat. We may need to wait for a bit before we get Wyn's attention." I complied, and when he pulled me tighter against his side, I didn't resist.

He withdrew a folded paper from his pocket and cupped it in both hands. After whispering something to it, he leaned over and let it flutter to the water.

I blinked at it. "Bryce gave you a paper boat?"

He chuckled. "What is it you human folk say? It's not the form that's important. It's the function. And I mind that your druid friend has a whimsical side to his nature."

That was true. Bryce had once configured a paintball tagger to deliver an anti-evil potion. I sighed as we watched the little white boat bob on the gentle swells, moving away from the dock as though it had an invisible paper motor. About ten feet out, it began to spin like it was caught in a tiny whirlpool and got sucked beneath the surface.

"Guess the message doesn't require a signature for delivery," I muttered.

Beside me, Lachlan uttered an odd sound, half cough, half hum, half throat-clearing. Okay, so fractions aren't my strong suit, but you get the picture. "Matthew."

When he didn't continue, I turned my head to look at him. He was staring out over the water, his brow knotted, and my belly felt as though it was trapped in that same mini-whirlpool. "Yes?"

"After Wyn surfaces, I won't be able to...be with you."

"Ah." The whirlpool spun faster. "I understand." But I didn't. Not really.

He must have caught my mood because he turned and took my hands, his face earnest in the sunlight reflecting off the lake. "Not forever. I don't mean that. But he and I will have meetings with the King's seneschal, with last affidavits to file and scheduling to finalize. Until we face the King and he severs our knot, our sundering won't be official." He smiled crookedly. "And I believe I've mentioned that I can't trust myself alone with you for too long."

The light dawned and my stomach stopped doing pirouettes. "Is that why you drove into town today? Why you brought Blair with you?"

"Aye. When Herne was able to give us Wyn's whereabouts, it got me thinking. I'll not risk your safety, not put you on the Wild Hunt's radar, even by association." His jaw tightened. "I'll not have our joining tainted by the least hint of wrongdoing."

I squinted at him. "When you say joining, do you mean *joining*? As in"—I gestured between us—"*joining*?"

His expression softened. "I do. In all senses of the word."

"Oh." I was trapped in that hot, dark gaze. "That's, um, good." Surely one kiss wouldn't be *that* risky. Lachlan's breath wafted over my cheek, my lips. *It's finally going to happen.* I leaned in, my eyelids fluttering as I closed that last. Critical. Inch.

And fell over sideways, because Lachlan surged to his feet. "Look!"

He pointed at the center of the lake, beyond where the boat had vanished. At first, as I pushed upright again, heat burning my cheeks above my beard, I thought he was just deflecting.

Redirecting to cover his sidestep of my awkward lunge, because all I could see was bright sunlight glinting on the greeny-blue water. But when I squinted against the glare, I realized the buttery yellow glow was coming from *below* the surface.

I pushed aside my embarrassment and scrambled up to stand next to Lachlan. This was it! After weeks of waiting and wondering, we were about to face Wyn again. I wasn't entirely sure whether I'd want to hug him or sock him when he showed up, because leaving Lachlan—and me—hanging was kind of a jerk move. But then, Wyn had been magically roofied by his douchebag of an ex-boyfriend, so I couldn't entirely blame him for wanting some space.

Lachlan fumbled for my hand, and I clutched his, almost leaning over the water as the glow floated closer...closer... closer. As it brightened, the dock began to vibrate, shivering on its pilings in time with an arhythmic drumming.

Then a furry white figure the size of a small pony shot by us, sending me stumbling against Lachlan. It landed in the lake with a massive splash that drenched the front of my jeans.

Lachlan wiped water off his face. "Is that—"

"It is," I said resignedly, as an enormous white dog with red ears flailed in the water in front of the dock. "Our very own hellhound." Which meant—

"Doop!" Jordan Tate, Quest's werewolf intern, raced down the dock to teeter on its edge until Lachlan grabbed his giant backpack to steady him. "Not the *water*. The *selkie*." He shot a grin at us. "Hi, Hugh! Hi, Lachlan. Sorry about the mess."

"Okay, Jordan. I'll ask the obvious question. Why are you here?"

"We're working on his tracking skills," he said, his attention on Doop. "I told him to find Lachlan, but he's having a hard time separating the person from the place. I probably need to be a little more specific, huh?" He shrugged off his pack. "His aim is still a little wonky too, but we're working on that with some

Frisbee therapy." Jordan kicked off his sneakers and shed his jacket.

When he unbuckled his belt, I said, "Hang on. What are you doing?"

He peered at me from under his floppy brown bangs. "I have to get him out of the water, obviously." He heaved a sigh as he looked at Doop, who was smacking the lake surface with his front paws in an extremely uncoordinated dog paddle. "Again."

"But you hate the water."

"I know. But Doop's my responsibility, so it's up to me, isn't it?" He shucked off his jeans, revealing a pair of *Avengers* briefs. "But that doesn't mean I want to walk around in wet clothes all day." He smiled sunnily. "Good thing I started carrying extra underwear in my pack after the last three times."

"Laddie," Lachlan said, "yon hellhound must weigh twice what you do. You'll not be able to lift him out on your own."

"I'm a werewolf. We're stronger than we look."

Lachlan lifted his brown henley and reached for his belt buckle, exposing a tantalizing glimpse of skin. "You'll need help."

"Whoa." I held my hands up in a timeout T, which unfortunately prompted Lachlan to drop his shirt hem. "Let's think about this a little, shall we?" I checked on Doop. He didn't appear to be in danger of drowning—the three of us were more threatened by the water he was flinging about than he was. Well, us and the lake's entire fish population. While he didn't look exactly ecstatic to be in the drink, he didn't look panic-stricken either. I pointed to the shore next to the dock. "Why not just call him from over there? Get him to come out on his own?"

Jordan froze with his hands on his T-shirt hem. "But he's not good at swimming." Understatement. "How can he get over there?"

I shrugged. "Entice him. Offer him a treat. It might take him a while, but he'll manage with the right incentive."

Jordan brightened. "That's a great idea, Hugh!" He caught the strap of his backpack and scampered up the dock in his T-shirt, socks, and briefs.

I sighed. "I suppose I should be grateful he didn't strip down completely this time."

Lachlan lifted that scarred eyebrow. "This time?"

"Long story." I poked him in the chest. "And don't pretend you weren't about to do the same."

"Just trying to help." He winked.

"Uh huh."

On the shore, Jordan unzipped the backpack and pulled out a Frisbee. Because of course he would.

"Here, Doop! Here, boy!" He waggled the bright green disk over his head. Doop uttered a yip and began thrashing toward the shore. "That's it. You can do it." Doop flailed harder, generating a veritable canine tsunami as he floundered toward shore.

When he finally heaved to his feet in the shallows and lolloped into Jordan's arms, I turned back to the lake.

The glow had vanished. Guess Wyn wouldn't be breaking the surface today after all.

Dammit.

CHAPTER THREE

Lachlan didn't have much to say on the drive back to Portland, not that he was ever particularly garrulous. But with Jordan sitting behind us in the extended cab, a towel-wrapped Doop draped across his lap, he was even less chatty.

"Thanks for the towel, Lachlan," Jordan said.

"No worries, laddie. I always keep a few spares in the truck."

"I guess I should start carrying one in my backpack until I can train Doop to stay out of the water."

I glanced back at him a little sourly. "Wouldn't it have been better to go back to the office through Faerie?"

Jordan shook his head. "The FTA drivers get freaked out by Doop. Every time I call one, they take one look at him, shriek, and disappear again." He wrinkled his nose. "It's bad enough that they charge me for a missed pickup." He leaned over Doop's back and whispered, "But it hurts Doop's feelings."

I studied the hound, who nearly filled the rear of the cab with no room to spare for Jordan, his eyes closed and the Frisbee under one paw. "Yeah. He looks devastated."

Jordan actually glared at me, although his teeth were chattering. In addition to being wet, Doop was also cold—all the *Cwn Annwn* were, like refrigerator cold. It was normal for them, but could be a problem for anybody in close proximity. "Hugh, he's *very* sensitive. Positive reinforcement is *crucial*."

I cranked up the heater. "Right. Sorry, Jordan." He narrowed his eyes at me and I sighed. "Sorry, Doop." The apology earned me a brilliant smile from Jordan, but not even a tail twitch from Doop. Apparently flailing around in lake water and scaring away a guy we'd been searching for since September really took it out of a pup.

Lachlan found a parking spot a couple of blocks away from the Quest offices. "Is it all right if I wait here with you until it's time for me to pick Blair up at the zoo?"

More time with Lachlan? Sign me up. "Sure. We've repurposed the third floor conference room for a staff break room, so you can hang out as long as you need to."

Extracting Doop from the cab was the usual production number, although he fit a lot better in Lachlan's truck than he did in my Honda. He gave Jordan a pitiful glance from under his tufted eyebrows when Jordan clipped a leash on him.

"Sorry, boy," he murmured. "Just until we get inside."

We trooped through the street-level doors into the inner vestibule, Doop sniffing interestedly at the aromas wafting from the falafel restaurant next door, and took the stairs to the Quest lobby on the second floor. Zeke was seated behind his desk. Our demon office manager was sweet and welcoming every day, but today, he was practically vibrating with excitement, his grin wide and his eyes sparkling behind the bespelled eyeglasses that let him see in the Upper World despite his Sheol-adapted sight.

Doop uttered a short bark and bounded over to plant his front paws on Zeke's desk and gift him with a doggy smile. Jordan claimed Doop's affection for Zeke was because he recognized a kindred spirit, another denizen of a hell-equivalent who was now following a different path. However, I suspected Zeke's role as the purveyor of all office treats had more to do with it, even though Jordan was the only one allowed to feed the hound. He'd made that very clear, scolding Eleri severely when she'd offered Doop a scone under the table.

"Doop! Down!" Jordan said firmly. And Doop obeyed.

Zeke rested his clasped hands on the desk top. "Well? Did it work?"

Ah. Of course. He knew all about our trip today. "Not entirely. There was definitely a response to the message charm, but then Doop made an unscheduled splashdown in the lake."

"I said we were sorry," Jordan said severely. "Positive reinforcement, Hugh."

Zeke's nose twitched. "Jordan, if you wouldn't mind taking Doop home and giving him a bath? I'm afraid his...aroma is a little strong, and we want the office to be welcoming."

"Sorry, Zeke." Jordan glanced at the carpet, which, like Zeke's desk, sported some muddy partial paw prints. "I'll clean that up when we get back."

Zeke waved it away. "Don't worry. I'll take care of it."

"Thanks, Zeke. You're the best! Come, Doop." With the hellhound still leashed, Jordan led him back downstairs and out onto the sidewalk.

"I still can't believe he can walk a dog that size through the Portland streets without anyone noticing," I said.

"Oh, the *Cwn Annwn* have their own sort of *glamourie* when they want," Zeke said. "Doop will look just like an ordinary dog to humans."

I raised an eyebrow. "I'm human, and he looks far from ordinary to me. He didn't look ordinary to Bob, either, when he spotted him outside those Burgervilles."

Zeke frowned thoughtfully. "With Bob, I think it was because Doop was so hungry and stressed. He didn't bother, or couldn't. I've been told that once a person sees the *Cwn Annwn* for what they truly are, they can never be unseen. The *glamourie* only works on strangers."

"Really? Hmmm." I pulled a palm-sized notebook, the one I used to record new facts about the supernatural world, out of my camera bag. "Do you think the hounds can turn the *glamourie* on at will? Can they control what kind of dog the other person sees? Could Herne, or whoever they recognize as an authority figure, command them to take on a certain appearance?"

Lachlan laughed. "Steady on. I'll wager poor Zeke doesn't have all the answers."

"No," I said with a sidelong glance at Lachlan, "but I'll bet Herne does. And since he said I could call on him whenever I needed to, maybe I can arrange a little chat to talk about hellhound abilities."

"You could," Lachlan said. "But you might want to keep the requests at a minimum. Herne might be grateful to you for your past service to him, but he's still a bloke with a chancy temper. If you—"

"Is this Quest Investigations?"

I turned at the imperious contralto voice. A woman a few inches taller than Eleri was standing in the lobby doorway. She was dressed in a conservatively cut gray-blue business suit and open-necked cream silk blouse. Green and blue stones sparkled in her necklace and in the drop earrings peeking through her peat-brown hair.

Nothing about her appearance, while neat and definitely upscale, was out of the ordinary for a Portland executive or socialite. At least nothing other than her hair. Because it was wet. Dripping wet, with droplets clinging to the curling ends, sparkling nearly as brightly as the jewels at her throat. Oddly, even though her hair lay over her shoulders, her suit jacket was completely dry. As I goggled at her, a drop fell off one curl, but it vanished before it hit the carpet.

Luckily, Zeke was more on the ball than I was. He smiled at her warmly. "Yes, indeed, madam. How may we help you today?"

The woman studied all three of us, her sharp-eyed gaze shifting from Zeke to me to Lachlan. "Just so," she murmured and paced across the carpet on sensible heels the same brown as Doop's muddy paw prints.

Lachlan and I both made way for her to stand in front of Zeke's desk. She had that effect. She was a good four inches shorter than me, not large or particularly imposing, but she had an *air* about her, if you know what I mean. Not authority, or at least not precisely. More that she had a very solid sense of *self*, and didn't need anybody else's approval, thank you very much.

"I have a…difficulty," she said, "and if I find you suitable, I may wish to engage your services."

Zeke's professional smile never wavered, although I bristled a little at the notion that Quest might be *unsuitable*. "Of course. I'd be happy to answer any questions you might have. If you—"

"What is your place here?" she asked me.

I was tempted to frown at the way she brushed Zeke aside, but hey, she was a potential client. "I'm Hugh Mann, surveillance specialist and one of Quest's investigators."

She smiled, showing a row of straight white teeth. "Hugh Mann, is it? A name as well as a label? I would prefer to know your actual name, if you please."

I glanced furtively at Zeke. There was no reason why our clients couldn't know my real name, but few of them cared. Lachlan, in fact, was the only former client who'd made a point of addressing me by anything other than my *nom de* Quest. "Matt. Matt Steinitz."

"Pleased to make your acquaintance, Mr. Steinitz." She turned to Lachlan. "And you?"

Lachlan wasn't as cowed by the lady as I was. He smiled, showing his own teeth. "My place"—he jerked his chin at me— "is with him."

She nodded, and I could swear I saw a glint of approval in her eyes. "Selkie and human. A fine traditional pairing." She turned to Zeke. "And you?"

"Oh." Zeke blinked, his pale face blotching with red in his version of a blush. "I'm, er, Zeke Oz. Office manager."

"Of Sheol, I believe?"

Zeke met her gaze squarely. "The Host is no longer relegated to any realm by law. I reside here in the Upper World now."

She inclined her head. "I meant no insult or disrespect."

"Since you know about us, might I please have your name and…nature?" Zeke indicated his computer. "For our records?"

She smiled, as regal as a queen. "You may call me Cerys. Cerys Glynn. I am of the *Gwragedd Annwn*."

Beside me, Lachlan sucked in a breath. "The lake ladies," he murmured. "Welsh fairy wives."

"Lake, yes," she said, amusement coloring her tone. "Or river. Although those other terms are far too age and gender restrictive. My kind is not only female, nor are we only adults and…spouses." She made a moue of distaste. "So much of our lore was transcribed by men in less enlightened times." She smiled at us benignly, but I got the impression that her backbone was forged of pure titanium. "So, just as the Host is no longer bound by archaic rules, let us abandon outdated nomenclature and assumptions, shall we?"

I shared a glance with Zeke. "Uh. Sure."

"Now," she said briskly, both hands clasping her leather clutch in front of her, "I would like to speak to the principal."

"I'm afraid you must be mistaken," Zeke said. "We're not a school. We're an investigation agency."

Another two drops of water fell from her hair and vanished as she regarded Zeke expressionlessly. "I am aware. I was referring to the person whose name is on your articles of incorporation. Your CEO. Your boss."

"Oh." Zeke blushed harder. "I'm sorry. I just took a call from an instructor at the supe school, so…" He nudged a Quest brochure across the desk. "We actually have two principals. Mal Kendrick and Niall O'Tierney."

"O'Tierney?" she said sharply. Her gaze lost focus as she stared at a spot on the wall over Zeke's desk. "I had no idea… But *Niall*, you say?"

"Yes." Zeke recovered his composure. "He and Mal are in conference at the moment, but they should be done shortly, if you'd like to take a seat. May I offer you tea? Coffee? Some other beverage?"

She nodded graciously. "Water would be lovely."

Zeke rose and stepped out from behind his desk, but paused at the hallway entrance. I could hear Mal's cheerful voice and Niall's laughter approaching.

"Oh." Zeke turned and smiled at Cerys. "Here are Mal and Niall now."

The two men entered the lobby. Although I was quite familiar with the mischief glinting in Mal's cobalt eyes, I'd never seen Niall looking quite so joyful. He practically glowed. The wedding plans must be going well. And before you ask, no, I wasn't envious. My day—*our* day—would come. I was sure of it.

"Now that you'll officially be my brother-in-law," Mal said, slapping Niall on the back, "I'll be able to really take the piss out of you. What's family for, eh?"

Niall rolled his eyes, clearly about to make a comment not suitable for client consumption, when he caught sight of Cerys. His eyes narrowed. Every bit of happiness vanished from his face until his clenched jaw resembled granite.

"Mal, Niall." Zeke stood aside and gestured to Cerys. "Allow me to introduce—"

"You!" Niall growled. "Get out."

CHAPTER FOUR

My mouth dropped open. So did Lachlan's, Mal's, Zeke's—heck, we looked like a school of carp.

"Niall?" Zeke said faintly. "This lady is a potential client. She has a case for us."

"No." Niall spun on his heel and stomped up the hallway. His office door slam made Zeke's keyboard rattle.

Mal cast a bewildered glance after his business partner. "What the flaming abyss?" He grimaced. "I expect I should see what's got his knickers in a knot." He smiled apologetically at Cerys. "We're not in the habit of turning away clients. It's in our charter with Their Majesties—we're obligated to assist any supe with a legitimate problem, as long as they're transparent with us and don't intend harm." He jerked his chin at Lachlan. "Ask him. I'd have turned him away if I'd had the choice."

Lachlan snorted. "I'd have stayed away myself if there'd been any other option." Then he smiled fondly at me. "Although things turned out much better than I'd had any right to expect."

"Too right." Mal held out his hand to Cerys. "Mal Kendrick."

"Yes. Your reputation, yours and your brothers', precedes you."

Mal grinned. "Don't hold that against me, all right? I've changed my ways now that I'm a married man. You are?"

She took his hand and Mal flinched, eyes widening. "Cerys Glynn.

"Of the *Gwragedd Annwn*," he muttered, staring at their joined hands. "And I know which one. Shite."

A smile glimmered on her lips. "Just so."

"Right, then." Mal let go of Ms. Glynn and clapped his hands once. "Zeke, please escort Ms. Glynn to the Little Conference Room and see that she's comfortable?"

"Of course." Zeke hurried over to her side. "If you would come with me, please? I'll get you your water, and if you like, I can arrange other refreshments as well."

She took Zeke's offered arm. "Lovely. Please lead on."

Mal waited until Zeke had led Ms. Glynn out of the lobby and up the stairs. Then he ran both hands through his hair and grimaced. "Shite. What a cock-up."

I raised my hand. "Excuse me? Would you like to share a little information with the class?"

Mal's expression turned sardonic. "The lovely lady no doubt noshing on scones upstairs is none other than the King of Faerie's long-lost mum."

My knees wobbled, and Lachlan steadied me with a hand under my elbow. "The King's *mother*? But she looks younger than me."

"She's fae, Hugh. She'll look youthful until the end." Mal glanced down the hallway toward his office. "Thank the Goddess that Eamon had already left. If you think Niall had a poor reaction, I imagine his might be worse."

"Wait a minute." I wish I had access to all the notes on my computer right this second. "Eamon's the elder brother and Niall's mother was human, right?" Mal nodded. "Was she legally married to the old king?"

Mal snorted. "Define legally. That bastard Tiarnach was old school that way. He never asked when he could take. He abducted Niall's human mother in the time-honored tradition of entitled fae everywhere. He had to work a little harder for Cerys, seeing as she's fae, too." He sighed, propping a hip on Zeke's desk. "Probably thought it was worth the effort."

I gazed thoughtfully at the archway that led from the lobby to the stairwell. "Well, she's pretty, but—"

"Tiarnach wouldn't work that hard for lust. He wasn't a bloke concerned much with consent when it came to sexual conquest. But the *Gwragedd Annwn* aren't just pretty faces." He rubbed his thumb and fingers together in the standard gesture for filthy lucre. "They've got dowries. Big ones. If he wanted her gold, he had to play nice, at least at the beginning. He might have even restrained himself for a while, if his greed outstripped his temper."

Lachlan shook his head. "From what I've heard, the old king wasn't one to deny himself anything. Believed he was entitled to anything he could grab, whether people, places, or things." He shook his head. "Folk are better off without kings. Too much power can twist a fellow's soul."

I studied Lachlan's somber expression. "Is that why you won't take the throne?" Did I mention? My almost-boyfriend is technically the selkie king, even though he refuses to rule.

Lachlan smiled at me. "Nay. In my case, it's because the selkie clans are too willing by half to let another make decisions for them. They like the notion of having somebody else to blame when things go wrong."

"Wonderful," I said faintly. "But that still doesn't explain why Tiarnach took a second wife when his first one was still alive and kicking. Did they sever the knot? A sundering, like you and Wyn?"

"You'll want your wee journal for this one, Matthew." Lachlan nodded at the notebook I still clutched in one hand. "The witches would approve of the *Gwragedd Annwn*."

"Are they witches too?"

"Nay. But their relationships are bounded by natural consequences."

I narrowed my eyes at him. "Still waiting for the shoe to drop."

"Stop edging him, Brodie." Mal crossed his arms. "What your stroppy wanker of a boyfriend is dangling in front of you like a promise of release is that if the *Gwraig Annwn's*—"

"Wait." I screwed up my face. "Sorry. But keeping track of Welsh words makes my head spin. You've called her a *gooreyeg* and a *grageth*. Which is it?"

Mal grinned. "Not a lot of Welsh words with Latin roots. One *Gwraig*. Two *Gwragedd*. Singular and plural."

I scribbled a note to have Eleri give me the actual spelling to go with the phonetic pronunciation later. "Thanks. You were saying?"

"If the lady's partner strikes her three causeless blows, she can leave the blighter in the dust, and take her dowry with her. Although if there are any children, they're left behind."

My pencil scratched a deep groove in the page. "I'm sorry, but what the hell?"

Lachlan frowned at me. "I know leaving the bairns behind is a great pity, but don't you think she'd be justified in taking her belongings with her?"

"That's not what I mean." I glowered at them. "*Causeless* blows? That presupposes that any blow someone lands on their partner could have any cause whatsoever. Who *makes* these rules?" As thrilled as I was by knowing the supernatural was real, sometimes the details really got in my hair, you know?

Mal smiled ruefully. "You'll need to take it up with the old gods, mate, and though you and Govannon are BFFs now—"

"We're not," I grumbled. "He just touched my chest, like, for a nanosecond."

"Ah, well." Mal pushed himself off the edge of the desk. "Then we're stuck with how things were laid down in the times before." He glanced down the hallway again, and it struck me.

"You're afraid to face him," I said. "Niall."

Mal scowled at me. "I'm not afraid. Exactly. But Niall's worst behavior has always been triggered by threats to one of two people, the two he holds more precious than his own hide: his own brother and mine. He'll do anything to protect Eamon or Gareth." He grimaced. "I'm just afraid he'll be willing to sacrifice Quest to settle a score that may not exist anywhere but in his own mind."

"Mal," I said gently, "putting it off won't make it easier. You need to talk to him."

"I know." He gazed at me with a twisted smile. "Will you think less of me if I confess I wish Bryce were here to hold my hand?" He wiped his palms along his thighs, and it caught me below the heart—the idea that Mal's palms were sweating at the notion of facing someone who was practically family. "But you're right. I can't put it off."

"If you need backup..." I spread my hands, palms up.

A relieved smile dawned. "Brilliant, mate. By all means, come along."

Lachlan slung an arm across my shoulders and tugged me against him. "If you're putting Matthew in danger—"

"Stow it, Brodie. We might need an impartial referee, and whatever else you are, you're not impartial, not where Hugh is concerned, and we don't need even more complications."

I turned to Lachlan and put my hand on his chest. "I appreciate your protectiveness, but this is my job. Your job is running fishing charters and"—I widened my eyes in a mock glare—"finding your husband so you can get fae-divorced before I register for Medicare."

"As to that—"

"Lachlan, please? I don't have time to brangle with you today, not when there's other brangling looming in the wings."

He ran a hand through his hair, a rueful smile on his broad, tanned face. "Aye. Sorry, lad." He traded glares with Mal—the kind they seemed to reserve only for each other—before covering my hand with his. "I have every confidence you're capable of keeping yon fae lordlings in line. I'll call an FTA driver and head back to that lake. Maybe the waters will have calmed enough for Wyn to surface by now." His gaze dropped to my mouth. *A kiss? Did he want it as much as I did?*

But then Mal cleared his throat, and Lachlan simply patted my hand. *Dammit.*

I tried not to show my disappointment—after all, this *was* my workplace and Mal *was* my boss. As unselfconscious as he and Bryce were about PDAs, I wasn't sure I was quite there.

Especially since Lachlan wasn't free yet.

"Depending on how this afternoon goes, I may be busy with this case tonight."

He nodded, and I hoped his smile was tinged with a little disappointment. "When I pick Blair up, should I tell Eleri to stop in?"

"No. Let her enjoy her day off." Especially if it meant she got to spend more time with her coffee shop crush. "I'll fill her in later."

With one last smile for me and a glare for Mal, Lachlan strode out of the lobby. I could hear his footsteps in their heavy boots on the stairs and sighed.

Mal chuckled. "I'd take the mickey out of you for mooning over your man, but I've got no room to talk." The mirth died out of his face, and his mouth settled into a grim line. "Come on. We'd best try to talk some sense into Niall."

"Think we'll manage?" I asked as we headed down the hallway.

He paused, his hand on Niall's office doorknob. "Not a chance in all the hells."

CHAPTER FIVE

When we walked into Niall's office, he was staring out the window, his back ramrod straight. When he didn't acknowledge us, Mal closed the door with a decisive click. When Niall still didn't react, Mal opened the door and closed it again with more force. Still nothing.

"Bloody stubborn git," Mal murmured. "Come on, mate. Time to stop sulking."

"I'm not *sulking*." With that growl, Niall could have passed for a troll or a duergar. He still didn't turn around.

Mal strolled in and leaned against the end of Niall's big oak desk. "You threw a tantrum in front of our client and ran away to hide in your room with a blanket over your head. Seems like sulking to me."

At that, Niall spun, and the expression on his face hit me like a blow to the chest, sending me backing up a step to thump against the door. "I. Am not. *Sulking*. You know who she is. You know what she did."

Mal, clearly made of sterner stuff than me, didn't bat an eye at Niall's fury. "I do. As much as anyone does. But I could point out that neither one of us were around at the time, so everything we know about the matter is hearsay."

"It's not *hearsay*." He jabbed a finger at Mal. I wasn't sure he'd even noticed I was in the room. "Look at the evidence and tell me she deserves anything but contempt."

"All right." Mal crossed his ankles, the picture of ease, but I knew better. "Hit me with it."

"She abandoned her son. You can't deny that. She left Eamon at Tiarnach's mercy. He was only eight years old and she *left* him there, in that joyless Keep."

"I think you're jumping to the end of the story, mate." Mal's voice took on a steely edge. "Tiarnach enticed her, lured her in. I expect you could check with the Keep staff to find out how—the lesser fae know everything, and they'd have had to prepare the offering." He snorted. "I can't see Tiarnach nipping down to the kitchen to bake bread or slice a nice wedge of cheese on his own."

"So? She didn't have to accept it, no matter how tasty." He spit out the last word. "She had a choice. She always had a choice."

"Did she?"

Niall took a step forward. "You're standing up for her just because she's *Welsh*. You Welsh fae have never gotten over your feud with the Irish back in Bran's day."

Uh oh. "Guys? Maybe we should leave ancient nationalism out of it?"

They ignored me. Mal pushed off the desk, his fists clenched. "You forget, O'Tierney—or should I say *MacTiarnach*—that I know who her husband was. I met him. He nearly broke Bryce's wrist. He nearly *ran him through*. Think what he'd do to a woman who was totally in his power, living in his Keep, surrounded by nobody but the *Irish*. Can you blame her for escaping?"

"Yes!" Niall roared. "Because she left Eamon behind! Her son. An innocent. At *his* mercy."

"Because he *hit her*!" Mal shouted back. "At least three times, you sod. She was *entitled* to leave."

"And you think he wouldn't take out his rage on Eamon?"

"I don't dispute that Eamon's childhood would have been difficult without his mother—"

"Difficult," Niall spat. "Easy for you to say. You never had a mother. You don't know what it does to a child to have her abandon you as if you meant nothing. You didn't even have a childhood. You—"

"Does my brother know you hold such a low opinion of *Welshmen*? Maybe I should drop him a hint before he's handfasted to you."

"My relationship with Gareth is none of your business."

"No? He's my *brother*. You lied to him, let him believe that lie and pine after you for two bloody centuries! I'm the one who had to hold him together, so don't tell me it's none of my business, not if you're planning to—"

I put two fingers in my mouth and whistled. "Guys? Time out. I think maybe we should take this down a notch." Or twenty.

They both glared at me. "This has nothing to do with you, Hugh," Niall said, his teeth clenched.

I approached them cautiously. "Actually, it does. You're letting old wounds get in the way of our mission. You said it yourself, Niall, when Bob the delivery guy—the *human* delivery guy—showed up in the office complaining about a giant spectral hound stalking his truck. The Quest spells are *inclusionary*. Regardless of what happened in the past, if Ms. Glynn didn't have a legitimate claim on Quest's aid, she could never have crossed the threshold." I nodded at Mal. "You said it a few minutes ago—we're *obligated* to assist her. It's as much a part of our mandate as searching for the Disappeared."

"I refuse to help the woman who abandoned my brother," Niall said stiffly.

"Fine. Mal can take the case."

"Oh no he can't," Niall said. "He's got Welsh bias. He'll take her part."

"Better than taking Tiarnach's part," Mal retorted.

I took a deep breath, reminding myself that clocking both my bosses with a paperweight would probably get me fired. "Since

A) Eamon isn't here, and B) Tiarnach is dead anyway, and C) we don't know what Ms. Glynn wants from us, both of you are being unreasonable. If Mal—"

"No," Niall said stubbornly. "Mal can't take the lead, and I won't touch her with a barge pole." He stared at me out of narrowed eyes. "*You* take the case."

My belly fluttered again. "Me?" Sure, I wasn't restricted to surveillance duty anymore and my *provisional* status with the supe council could be counted in days, not weeks, but clearly this case came with a lot of emotional baggage for both my bosses. "Are you sure?"

Niall said, "No," at the same time Mal said, "Yes."

I rolled my eyes. "Niall, *you're* the one who suggested it. Did you change your mind already?"

"I don't want *Quest* to take the case," he said sullenly. "But if anybody's going to do it, it should be you and your team."

My belly added a backflip to its flutter. "My team?"

For an instant, Niall's face cleared of anger and misery, replaced with sardonic amusement. "If you try to convince me that you won't involve Eleri and Jordan—and where Jordan goes, Doop goes—I won't believe you. Nor that Lachlan Brodie won't stick his flipper in too, if it looks like you're having problems."

Wow. I guess I did have a team.

"But I'm warning you, Hugh," Niall said, morphing back to ragey angst, "if she jeopardizes Eamon's happiness in *any way*, not only will her case be terminated, but your employment will as well. Get it?"

I swallowed. "Got it."

He nodded decisively. "Good."

Despite the warning, though, my spirits lifted considerably. While I'd been the primary investigator on Lachlan's case back in September, Mal had still been the lead. But this time, *I* was the lead. My first solo case! Well, solo along with my *team*, but my team was awesome, so I could live with that.

"I'll get right on it." I turned to go, but then something struck me. "Niall, if you—"

"I can't stay here," he muttered. "Not with her in the building." He glared at Mal. "And you keep your nose out of it too."

Mal crossed his arms and glared back. "All I want is for our process to be fair and impartial."

"Impartial." Niall snorted. "Right. You've never been—"

"Guys." I dared to step between them, because even though they were both high fae with major magic at their disposal, they'd never set anybody on fire. That I knew of. "Seriously. You both need to stand down. It's my case now. I'll handle it."

Niall simply grunted and strode out of the room. Unlike Mal, he had no qualms about slamming the door behind him.

Once he was gone, Mal visibly deflated. "Shite," he muttered. "Nothing like a couple of millennia of resentment to make a bloke unreasonable."

I stared at the door. "Where's he gone, do you think?"

"Probably to Gareth. The band's rehearsing in LA today, so he can sit in the corner and brood to his heart's content."

"Could I ask a question?"

Mal winced. "Hells, Hugh. We're not mad at *you*. Ask whatever you want." He smiled crookedly. "After all, you're the lead investigator."

I was, but I wasn't sure exactly what Niall expected me to accomplish. Did he *want* me to solve Ms. Glynn's case, whatever it was? Or had he handed it to me because he thought I was the most likely to screw it up?

I tried to push that second notion away. Both Niall and Mal had always claimed they didn't see me as *less* because I was human. That in fact they'd lobbied for me to join Quest in the first place. But when—as Mal said—centuries of *feelings* were involved, I wasn't sure I could count on either of them being completely clear-sighted.

I flipped to a clean page in my notebook. "As I understand it, the King is the elder brother, correct?"

Mal nodded. "Yes."

"I get that the old king was a piece of work, but did he have two wives or consorts or whatever at once?"

"No. For whatever reason, he only had one official consort at a time, whether they were technically there by consent or not." Mal snorted. "I don't think it was from any notion of propriety or personal restraint. Tiarnach was a self-centered arsehole who cared about nothing but himself. I think having a single consort at a time was simply his inability to multi-task."

"Okay. But if Ms. Glynn was gone before Tiarnach married Niall's mother—"

"Kidnapped her, you mean."

"Kidnapped, then. How did Niall recognize Ms. Glynn before she ever said her name?"

Mal sighed. "Eamon had a portrait of her. A miniature that he kept as one of his most treasured possessions. He showed it to Niall often when they were boys, especially after Niall's own mother died, probably spinning tales of how one day she would return and take them both away. Tiarnach discovered it when Niall was about eight and Eamon sixteen. He burned it and made them both watch. Then he beat the hells out of both of them for betraying him."

"Crap," I murmured.

"As you said, he was a piece of work."

I studied him through narrowed eyes. "Call me suspicious, but I'm guessing neither Niall nor Eamon shared this little tidbit with you."

"Nah." Mal's smile this time was closer to his usual cocky mischief. He tapped his temple. "But the lesser fae see everything. And there's nothing fae love more than a good gossip with a friend."

CHAPTER SIX

When I walked back into the lobby, Jordan was sitting behind Zeke's desk, Doop on the floor next to him. If it weren't for the dog's lolling tongue, he'd look as regal as a New York Public Library lion, his fur fluffy and blinding white. The air was redolent with the scent of...bubble gum?

I raised my eyebrows. "Using kid's shampoo for Doop's bath?"

He wrinkled his nose. "He doesn't like the dog shampoo at the pet store."

"He doesn't or you don't?"

He widened his eyes. "Have you *seen* the ingredients on some of those? I bet they do *animal testing*!"

"And other pharmaceutical companies don't?"

"I didn't get it from the store, anyway. I asked Dr. MacLeod to make it special, and he and his students cooked it up as a lab project, using only natural ingredients like fruits and essential oils and stuff." He beamed. "It's Doop's *signature* line!"

"Are they marketing it as *Hellhound Herbals*?"

"Shhh!" He glanced at Doop, whose head had dropped onto his paws, his eyes closed. "We don't use the H-word around him."

I frowned. "I thought it was okay now. A badge of honor, since he'd actually, you know, gone to hell."

Jordan gazed up at me seriously. "Positive reinforcement, remember? Since he's living away from the rest of Herne's pack, I don't like to use purge... prej... loaded words around him."

"Okay, okay. I'll try to watch my language." I gestured to the desk. "Covering for Zeke?"

He nodded enthusiastically. "I'm doing a regular shift now, so Zeke can handle other things."

"Is he still upstairs with the client?"

"Yep. In the Little Conference Room. But he's taking the afternoon off to sit in on a Hunter's Moon rehearsal." His face took on a wistful cast. "The band is working on a new song, one Gareth and Josh wrote about Zeke and Hamish."

I blinked. "Really? That's...incredibly romantic."

"I know, right?" He sighed. "I wish somebody would write a song about me. Although I'd probably have to find a boyfriend first, or it would be pretty depressing."

I could relate, although at least I had my boyfriend identified. I spared a moment to hope Lachlan was having better luck fishing Wyn out of the lake this afternoon than we'd had this morning.

I jerked my thumb at the ceiling. "I'm going up now." I couldn't help a little swell of pride as I said, "Niall and Mal have handed this case to me." Nobody needed to know that it was by default, right?

"That's awesome, Hugh! Congratulations!"

I was tempted to tell him that he was on my *team*, but until I knew more about the case, I didn't want to either get Jordan's hopes up or give him more time to think up completely inappropriate ways to "help." So I just grinned at him before heading up the stairs.

Apparently, Ms. Glynn had opted for something other than water, because when I walked into the conference room, Zeke was pouring her a cup of tea from the vintage Alice in Wonderland pot. While Zeke took his hospitality services seriously, he'd begun indulging in a surprisingly whimsical side and collecting quirky teapots and cups. He smiled at me as he set a plate of pastries next to her place. He'd already arranged a fresh notepad and several pens at my spot, so I set my notebook on the credenza, the better to keep my personal notes separate from the investigation.

"I'm so sorry to keep you waiting, Ms. Glynn." I sat across from her and picked up a pen. "I'll be handling your case for Quest."

"Please. Call me Cerys." She tilted her head to one side, and a droplet fell from one curl, *almost* making it to the table before it vanished. "Am I worthy of engaging your valuable services, then?"

I decided that neither defending Niall nor condemning his behavior would be conducive to a cordial client-investigator relationship, so I sidestepped the question. "Perhaps you could tell me a bit more about your difficulty?"

She sat back in her chair, her tea cup cradled in hands that looked more fragile than the china, studying me out of grave gray-blue eyes. "What do you know of my kind?"

Was this a test? Or did she sincerely want to give me new information? "I know that you're fresh water based. That you're one of the few supes whose relationships with humans is sanctioned."

"Sanctioned? Is that what they're calling it?" She took a sip of tea. "You mean our engineered vulnerability is codified into law."

I blinked. "Uh…"

She set down her cup with a clink. "Tell me, Mr. Steinitz"—I blinked again at her use of my real name—"if a person has, shall we say, diplomatic immunity, protected by law from being prosecuted for certain crimes, does that make the perpetration of those crimes any less despicable?"

"No."

"Countenancing the mating of humans and my kind doesn't protect *us*. That exception merely nods at the spell that puts us at risk of exploitation." She snorted. "Bread and cheese. Did you know? All that anyone—whether human or supernatural—needs to trap us is a bit of bread and cheese."

"Well, that sucks," I muttered, causing Zeke to drop a teaspoon.

She chuckled softly. "As you say. That may be why our method of leaving was also woven into our making, although once again, it deprives us of choice."

"You mean the three causeless blows thing?" I tapped my pad with my pen. "If you ask me, that's even more screwed up. I mean, your partner is allowed to hit you as long as it's for *reasons*? There *is* no reason for hitting your partner!"

She smirked. "I knew I liked you."

"So is that your…difficulty? An abusive partner?"

"Not precisely." She gazed into her tea cup as another drip didn't land. "I want you to find my child."

The belly flutter that had been constant since I'd been handed the case gave one last twitch and died. While I was glad Cerys wasn't being abused—at least at the moment—I had hoped for a slightly bigger challenge to prove myself. But if all she needed was to meet with the King? Yeah, it might be a little tricky, given the family drama I'd already witnessed, but it wasn't exactly hard to *find* him.

But she was fae, so shouldn't she know about him, anyway? Had she been hiding out under her lake and missed the last couple of years' worth of Faerie news flashes? Did she just need me to broker a meeting? I was a photographer and a fledgling investigator. Negotiations weren't exactly my strong suit. Or any suit, for that matter, but I could give it a shot.

"I believe," I said slowly, "that the King is in the Keep at the moment. He keeps regular hours in his audience chamber. If you'd like—"

She frowned at me. "Do you need royal permission to assist me in this matter?"

"No. But you said you wanted to find your child. The King is your son."

She waved a hand. "Not *that* child. I know where he is. I meant the other one."

CHAPTER SEVEN

I may have goggled at her. "You and Tiarnach had another child?"

Her mouth tightened in distaste. "No, thank the Goddess. But Tiarnach was not my only...partner."

I rubbed my eyes. "Okay. When you left Tiarnach and Eamon behind—"

Her eyes blazed, exactly like the glow under the lake. "You mean when Tiarnach struck me for the third time and I was forced to go."

I blinked. "You mean after the third blow—"

"After the third blow, we *must* go, returning to our lake or river, with all our riches." She laughed mirthlessly. "Do you forget the time of our coming, the world where we were made? Our goods, our livestock, whatever gold and jewels we bring as our dowry belong to us. But children?" The eye-glow died and her expression turned bleak. "Children belong to their *fathers*. Even if I had wanted to take Eamon with me—and I did, for I knew what Tiarnach was like, none better—I could not."

"Holy crap," I breathed. Why didn't Niall know about that? Why didn't Eamon? It would have made his childhood, if not merry, at least less miserable from a sense of abandonment. "Are these facts well known?"

Her lips quirked up. "To know, one must ask, and so few ever bother."

I thought of Grizel, the bean-nighe who'd given me grief for trying to finagle information out of her, and winced. She'd told me in no uncertain terms to *ask* rather than *take*. That seemed to be a theme with a lot of supes. The lore spelled out ways to trick or destroy them, but was seriously lacking in tales from their perspective.

"I should tell you that my boss is the King's brother, and he has some, er, *feelings* about you leaving Eamon at the mercy of Tiarnach."

"I suspected as much when you told me his name." She gazed into her teacup, turning it in her hands. "I did miss Eamon," she murmured. "I used to watch him from under the water when he played on the shore until Tiarnach forbade him from coming." She glanced up at me. "Bread and cheese can only lure us once. He tried to entice me with my son, but no matter how much I wanted to return, or to take Eamon away with me, I could not. My nature prevented it."

My ears burned like they always did when anger got the better of me. "So what you're saying is that the elder gods engineered your kind with a reverse restraining order?"

She nodded. "That is a modern way to refer to it, but yes."

Good grief. The elder gods were definitely graduates of the School of Punitive Management. Heck, they'd probably founded the damn thing—and didn't much care who bore the brunt of the punishment. I jabbed my pen on the notepad, over and over, frowning. "Is there a time limit on it? I mean, the King's been an adult for a couple of thousand years, as I understand it, and Tiarnach's, well, dead. Is there some reason you couldn't contact Eamon before now?"

Her cheeks grew pink and she cut a glance to the side. "Not now," she said, her voice barely audible. "Nothing other than shame or guilt. But not long after Tiarnach forbade Eamon from visiting the lake, I was enticed by another." She sighed. "I admit I let it happen, from grief over losing my son. I could have hidden more safely. Annwn wasn't closed to us in those days, although Arawn, its lord, adhered far too strictly to the old ways than was comfortable." She smiled wryly. "He would have turned a blind eye had twenty men cast out lures, one after the other."

I scowled at my notes. I'd heard about Arawn, the guy who'd literally lorded it over the Welsh fae in the past. According to Niall, he was the one responsible for Gareth's major trauma: being schooled by a ghost bard who'd been no prize even when he was alive. From all I'd heard, everyone was lucky Arawn *had* disappeared, taking the keys to Annwn with him.

"If you don't mind my asking"—I met her eyes again—"why not contact him now? You know where Eamon is. Tiarnach is gone." I gestured to her business suit. "You don't appear to be, er, bound to anybody at the moment." I eyed the cheese pastry on the plate at her elbow. "Unless it's to Zeke for serving you a Danish."

At the credenza, Zeke dropped an entire handful of silverware with a clatter. Cerys shot him a bemused glance. "Since his intent was not to coerce me into a conjugal union"— Zeke squeaked and hurried out of the room—"you need not fear any awkward repercussions. I..." She glanced out the window, biting her lip. "I know I should reach out to Eamon. But so much time has passed. And judging from his brother's reaction, he has neither forgiven nor forgotten."

"Listen." I leaned forward. "I know it's been a while, but Eamon's not a vindictive guy. He's happily married. Looking out for his subjects, whether they were originally Seelie or Unseelie. Working on bringing all fae into the twenty-first century and shaking off the cobwebs of some of those old traditions. Did you know Tiarnach cursed him? For like two hundred years?"

She reared back in her chair, eyes swirling with gold. "How *dare* he? If he weren't already dead, I'd—"

"Whoa." I dropped my pen and held up both hands. "It's been taken care of, but my point is that Eamon put up with a lot for the sake of his people, his brother in particular. What's the worst that could happen? You reach out to him and he rebuffs you." I shrugged. "Trust me, there's worse family drama in about 80 percent of most human households. But best case? You'll have your son again, who's a pretty staunch advocate for fae rights."

She still looked doubtful, but at least she didn't say flat no. Score one for the token human. I hadn't watched countless hours of *Lucifer* without picking up a few pointers on supernatural therapy. I held my breath until she nodded.

"Very well. I will consider it. But it must wait. As you say, Eamon is well and happy. The same is not true for my missing child."

Right. Before my little detour into DIY family therapy, we were actually discussing a case, a case that fell squarely within Quest's mandate. I mean, a missing child? Can't get more Disappeared than that. "Tell me about this kid. Can you give me a description?"

She met my gaze squarely. "No."

I blinked. "Okay. What gender expression?"

"I don't know."

"How old are they?"

"I don't know."

I forbore from snapping my pen in half. "You realize that if you expect me to find someone, I need to know who to look for."

"You misunderstand. It's not that I don't wish to tell you, it's that I cannot. I don't know what they look like. My child was taken from me, from Faerie, when I'd only just given birth. I never saw the babe, no more than I saw my husband after he stormed past the midwife and slapped me across the face three times."

I goggled at her. "You'd just given birth to his child and he *hit* you?"

Her smile was tight. "I suspect that he'd been paid well to do so. Well enough to offset his losses when I disappeared with my dowry."

I stared at her, nonplussed. "Tiarnach." It wasn't a question.

She inclined her head. "I believe so. He was like a dog worrying a bone, obsessed over perceived slights to his authority or worse, his wealth. I may have been gone, and he may have forgotten me as a person, but he never forgot what I brought to his coffers, and what I took with me when I left."

"Did he contact you then? Try to negotiate?"

"No." Her wide brow knotted with a frown. "I had assumed I had simply made another dismal choice in accepting a…a…"

"Cheese board proposal?" I offered.

"A partnership," she said severely.

"So let me retarget my earlier question. Why now? You've been forced to leave children behind before—the King being a case in point. What makes finding this one suddenly urgent?" I offered a clenched-jawed smile. "And please don't say you don't know."

She chuckled, although she cut another glance at the door. "I was contacted by an oracle."

"An oracle." I knew those were around. One of the doctors at St. Stupid's, the supe hospital, was an oracle, and the most insufferable know-it-all you'll ever meet. On the other hand, the manager for Hunter's Moon was an oracle too, and they were totally great. "Could you share their name?"

"That's irrelevant. Suffice it to say that their visions are reliable. They informed me that if I didn't locate my child before the next full moon, then…"

I waited, but she didn't go on. "Then what?"

She shrugged. "They didn't say. Only that locating my child was the key to preventing great harm."

"I don't suppose they specified whether this impending harm was bigger than a breadbox or could dance on the head of a pin? Or cause the extinction of all life as we know it?"

"While the oracle's visions are reliable, they are not always rife with detail. Let us say that I took the warning seriously enough to come here and seek your aid." She glanced at the door again. "Although I confess I had not anticipated the reception I received."

I winced. "Sorry about that. Like I said, Niall's got *feelings* where Eamon's well-being is concerned."

She frowned, tapping a fingernail—no polish, but buffed to a shine—against her tea cup. "If I had known Tiarnach had enticed another of my kind to the same fate—"

"Oh, Niall's mother was human." I grimaced. "Tiarnach courted her in the usual way."

She lifted a brow. "You mean he blinded her with *glamourie* and abducted her."

"Pretty much, yeah."

"Am I allowed to say that I'm glad that he's dead?"

"Can't say I'd want to run into him in a dark alley. You won't find anyone at Quest who's exactly sorry about the Faerie regime change either."

She shifted her gaze to the empty doorway again. "Can I ask how he met his end?"

"That was, ah, Herne's doing." I swallowed, still a little queasy over the whole Wild Hunt scenario, particularly the part where the *Cwn Annwn* might or might not consume the flesh of traitors. "Eamon summoned him by sounding the horn, but Herne and the pack took care of the details." I swallowed thickly. "Which I'm just as happy not to know about."

Her lips tilted in a slight smile, although her gaze never left the door. "I must remember to thank Herne one day. And I"— her smile gained teeth—"would revel in the details."

"Yes. Well." I cleared my throat. "Back to the... Do you need more tea?"

She tore her gaze away from whatever was so fascinating about the empty doorway. "I do not, thank you."

"Another pastry?" Although there were still several on the plate.

Her brows drew together. "No. Why do you ask?"

"You keep staring at the door. I figured you needed something from Zeke."

"Not Zeke. But when will the selkie be joining us?"

"Lachlan? Lachlan's not on the Quest staff. He's my boyfriend." Heat rushed up my throat at her narrow-eyed glare. "Well, my almost-boyfriend. It's complicated. But we've got an understanding. It's not a secret. I mean, we're not *hiding* it from anybody, we're just not..." What the heck was I doing? I didn't need to justify myself or divulge the details of my relationship to Cerys. For one thing, it was nobody's business but mine and Lachlan's. And, well, Wyn's too, I supposed, but only peripherally since he'd already opted out of the relationship emotionally if not technically.

"But..." She frowned at the door once more, as if scowling at it would cause Lachlan to manifest. Which, if that was a thing that could happen, I really needed to learn how to do. "The only reason I followed him here was because—"

"Wait." I grimaced. "I'm so sorry for interrupting, but do you mean you didn't arrive here at Quest because of our reputation? Because we're the only supe investigative service on the planet?"

"Of course not. I'd never heard of Quest before I walked through the doors."

CHAPTER EIGHT

"Y-you'd never heard of Quest?" Well, talk about a branding fail. We needed to do some serious PR and marketing work. Maybe Jordan could— Nope. Strike that. I'd ask Zeke to handle it while Jordan manned the phones. "You followed us from the lake?"

She set her half-empty cup in its saucer with a faint *clink*. "I followed the selkie. Lachlan, you said his name was? I could tell when I spied him through the water that he'd intentionally sought my child. I may not know my child's age, gender expression, or appearance, but he does."

I tried to ignore the sinking feeling in my belly. I had a sneaking suspicion I knew exactly who her "child" was. "Could I ask you something?"

"Of course."

"Is a *Corlun Dwr* related to a *Graig Annwn*?"

She waved one hand. "All Welsh water fae have much in common. *Corlun Dwr* is a more generic term. You could say that I'm a *Corlun Dwr*, but I'm also a *Graig Annwn*."

"Like all pines are trees, but not all trees are pines?"

"Exactly."

Crap. "So that was you? The glow under the water at the lake? You were responding to the little boat spell?"

She smiled, and for the first time she actually looked pleased and not as though she were simply being polite. "Yes. It was an elegant piece of work. Cross-dimensional. Quite lovely. That's why I decided to surface to see who'd sent it. But when I saw the selkie—saw Lachlan—I knew." She pressed a hand under her breasts, over her *calon*, the extra organ all supes had, the one that was the seat of their nature. "He's the key to finding my child."

"So..." I doodled on my pad—a shark fin cutting through waves. "While you were under the lake, did you, well, notice anybody else chilling down there?"

She frowned. "No. There had been a lot of activity on the surface over the last few days. Young beaver shifters are a trifle rambunctious. Any under-lake dwellers who valued their privacy would have retreated to stiller waters."

"But you were there?"

She shrugged. "I was there and not there. As I said, the spell was cross-dimensional. All lakes have the same heart. Those of us who know the trick can traverse from any of them to another."

Great. Not only had Herne's directions become obsolete before we ever got to Lake of the Beavers, but if what Cerys said was right—and I had no reason to doubt her—Wyn could flit from any given body of fresh water to another in a flick of his fins. Or whatever. Did *Corlun Dwr* transform when they were underwater, or did they just look like any random freediver?

"Could you excuse me for a moment?"

At her gracious nod, I scuttled out of the room and hurried down the curving corridor until I was out of sight of the door before I pulled out my cell phone. I dialed Lachlan's number, and he picked up immediately.

"Matthew." His voice was warm and that burr in his voice when he said my name hit me in the feels as usual. "I was thinking about you just now."

"You were?" I croaked.

"I'm always thinking about you."

"G-good to know. Say, are you still at the lake?"

He grunted. "Nay. The beaver kits were abroad again. I'm at the zoo, waiting for Blair. If we're not to anger their father, I'll need to get them home in good time."

"How soon could you get back here?"

"Not for two hours or more. I can't take Blair through Faerie. I've got to drive them home first. But I could take the FTA to your office if you need me."

I leaned against the wall. "Please. We need to talk."

"Matthew—"

"Remember that client? The lady with the wet hair who showed up before you left?"

"Aye." He sounded cautious and a little confused. Which was understandable.

The lump in my throat threatened to choke me. "She wants to speak with you."

"With me? Why?"

"Because…" I slid down the wall to butt plant on the gleaming tile floor. "Because I think she's looking for Wyn."

CHAPTER NINE

Cerys had wanted to wait for Lachlan to return, but I convinced her to schedule an appointment for later. She'd pushed for tomorrow, but I had severe doubts over whether we'd have any results for her, given my suspicions of her child's identity. Which, by the way, I hadn't mentioned to her. So I put her off for three days, letting her know that we'd contact her if we had news any sooner.

I suspected Eleri would call me craven or cowardly for failing to mention that I might have a lead. I preferred to think of it as cautious. For one thing, we'd been singularly unsuccessful at locating Wyn so far, and he might not even be her child.

Who was I kidding? He was totally her child. I was positive. It's not like Lachlan had been out searching for a dozen other water-based fae. In fact, he'd been doing his best to avoid them, at least when it came to the salty side of the family.

I was comforted at least that we probably wouldn't be bringing Cerys news that her child had passed of natural causes in London, or Tokyo, or Vladivostok ten, twenty, or two hundred years ago. Jeez, the time differential between Faerie and the Outer World made my head spin sometimes.

After seeing her out the door, I tromped back upstairs into the lobby. Jordan, for a wonder, didn't say anything as I paced back and forth in front of the reception desk, even though he and

Doop followed my progress like they were watching a one-sided tennis match.

Zeke edged back into the room with the plate of leftover pastries after I'd been muttering to myself for about ten minutes, although he just quietly took his place behind the desk, Jordan scrambling out of the chair to make room for him and perch on his usual stool against the wall.

"Oak and ash." Eleri appeared in the doorway, fists propped on her hips. "Who died?"

I shot an irritated glance at her. "Nobody yet. At least not as far as I know. Although Niall may be plotting some arcane Irish vengeance as we speak."

She perked up. "Really?" She strolled over and selected a cranberry-orange scone. "Do tell." Doop heaved to his feet and sniffed at her boots. She pointed a finger at him, leaves sprouting from its tip—but no thorns, I was relieved to see. "Don't even *think* about it, hound."

"He wouldn't," Jordan protested, as Doop flopped down and dropped his head on his paws, sighing heavily. "We've covered proper leg-lifting protocols already. He'd *never* pee on a friend."

"If you say so," she muttered.

"I don't think Niall would do anything *violent*, Hugh." Zeke folded his hands on his desk, his expression earnest. "It was just a shock."

"He's had shocks before, though." Jordan took two scones, much to Doop's interest. "Remember that time in Sheol when Hugh disappeared? He was plenty shocked then, but he didn't do anything other than yell at Lachlan for not holding on to you."

"Wait. *Niall* yelled at Lachlan?" That was usually Mal's MO. Well, not yelling so much as snarking and sniping.

"Only a little," Jordan said. "And I think Lachlan felt bad about it anyway because he didn't yell back."

Eleri plopped into a chair and nudged my calf with a booted toe. "Sit down, Hugh, before you make Jordan seasick."

"Hey! I don't get seasick!" He considered this for a moment, a scone suspended in one hand until Doop whined. "Sorry, boy." He broke off a corner of the scone and passed it to the hound. "At least I don't think I do."

Eleri smiled indulgently at him. "Never been on a boat, Jordan?"

He shuddered. "No! I can't figure out why anybody would leave the perfectly safe land. I mean, it's worse than dangling off a cliff. The bottom is farther away and there's all kinds of stuff in between that would kill you before you even landed. At least the ground doesn't try to smother you."

"Most of the time," I muttered, a certain incident with animate mud monsters far too fresh in my memory.

Jordan's eyes widened. "What?"

"You were there, Jordan. Do I need to remind you of the golems?"

"Oh, that." He waved one hand, scattering crumbs which Doop obligingly handled. "I can dig out from under dirt. I can't dig out from under water."

Eleri dusted off her fingers. "I still don't know what's going on and Hugh still hasn't sat down. So let's take care of both of those little issues, shall we?"

"Fine." I was tired of pacing anyway, and Zeke was eyeing the carpet as though I'd wear it out. I dropped into the chair next to Eleri. "Why are you in such a good mood, anyway?"

She grinned at me. "I just had a wonderful day. We had a great time at the zoo. Blair got along with Sassy's niblings, and we even ran into a bunch of kids on a field trip from the supe school who were about the same age." She chuckled. "They all had lunch together. Sierra, Sassy, and I had to drag them away to catch the elephant herd squishing some truly massive pumpkins."

I ignored most of Eleri's word dump to focus on the pertinent piece of information. "Who's Sassy?"

"Sierra's girlfriend." She wrinkled her nose. "Well, ex-girlfriend. Mostly. But she and Sierra are still friends."

I lifted an eyebrow. "That's sounding a lot like my situation with Lachlan."

She glared at me. "They're not *married*. They never were and hadn't ever planned to be. But they're fun, and trust me." She rolled her eyes. "With my OG clan chief and his petrified notions, I can use all the fun I can get."

When Eleri calls her clan chief OG, she doesn't mean Old Guard. She means Old Growth. The guy is a throwback to the days of total species separation. Unlike Eleri and her dryad "book club," he has zero sense of humor. Although considering the book club is far too fond of practical jokes at my expense, I suppose I should be glad that I'm not targeted by the humorless contingent as well.

"We're fun," Jordan piped up.

She smiled at him. "Well, at least you're never boring." She nudged my knee this time. "Come on, Hugh. Give."

"I've got my first solo case," I said glumly.

She sat up. "That's great! That must mean Mal and Niall trust you completely. I knew it had to happen sooner or later, especially considering how well you did rescuing Herne from those jackasses in Sheol."

"Yeah, I don't think that's entirely the reason." I sighed. "I'm not even sure I'm supposed to solve the case."

She frowned. "This isn't like the deal with Bob the delivery driver, is it? Humoring some potential client because the bosses don't really believe there's an issue?"

"Oh, there's an issue all right," I said. "But the issue is with Niall. Mal, too, but mostly Niall." I slumped further down in my chair until my butt was on the edge of the seat. "The client is the King's mother."

She stared at me, mouth agape—in other words, exactly the reaction all of us had when Niall had his little tantrum. "Shut up. Really? Like Niall's stepmother?"

"No. Eamon's the elder brother. So Niall's mother would have been *his* stepmother, assuming that even works in Faerie."

She shrugged. "Sometimes. Also, there's the whole time runs differently here, so she *could* have been Niall's stepmother depending on when and where people popped in and out of Faerie."

"Don't." I clenched my eyes shut and pinched the bridge of my nose. "Faerie timelines already make me dizzy. And besides, you told me that time doesn't move backwards, not even there."

She shrugged. "Not usually. But I've heard that a time surfer could change an event if they worked at it. It's not easy, but it could happen."

I peered at her out of narrowed eyes. "At some point, I want to find out more about time surfing, but that time is not now. Even assuming the fewest number of complications, this situation is still...still..."

"Complicated?" Jordan asked.

I gave him a half-hearted thumbs-up. "But whether Cerys Glynn is or is not Niall's stepmother, he definitely sees her as wicked, since she abandoned Eamon to Tiarnach's tender mercies when he was only a kid. Furthermore, when Mal pointed out that she wouldn't have made it through the door if she didn't have legit business with us, Niall practically accused him of blind Welsh fae nationalism."

"I take it Ms. Glynn is Welsh fae?"

I nodded. "*Gwraig Annwn.*"

She whistled through the slight gap in her front teeth. "The legendary ladies of the lake."

"Not only ladies, apparently, and not only lakes."

"Does she want to broker a meeting with the King then?"

"Nope. Not even a little bit." I grimaced. "To be honest, I'm not sure how that would go, although I think I ought to try eventually, if only for the sake of Niall's family damage. But she wants us to find her missing kid." When Eleri opened her mouth to state the obvious, I held up a hand. "Her *other* missing kid. And the thing is? I think the missing kid in question is Wyn."

She cocked her head. "What makes you think that? Kind of coincidence, don't you think?"

"Not really. We only caught her attention when Lachlan launched the spell to contact him. She followed the charm back and spotted Lachlan as the key." I swallowed thickly. "She said she could tell he sought her child. It's not like he's been looking for anybody else, other than…" I frowned. Wait a minute. Could it be? "Eleri, you can spot another supe, right?"

She nodded. "Some more easily than others, either the ones with an affinity for dryad nature, like earth and water-based folk—or those in opposition." She scowled. "Fire, for instance. Air and spirit, not so much."

"Could… Do you think Blair could be…" I gestured vaguely with one hand. "You know, a possible water baby?"

Her eyebrows shot up. "Blair? No. Nonbinary people have their own special magic, but I didn't get even a whisper of a calon tickle from them."

Dammit. It would have been so much better if Blair were the child in question, not only for my case's sake but for the kid's sake as well. Even a mother who lived under the nearest convenient lake would be a step up from Floyd.

"Since I'm the only other person Lachlan's, er, *sought* recently, and *I'm* certainly not her kid, there's only one other option."

"Wyn," she said with a wince.

"Yup."

"If I could make a suggestion?" Zeke said diffidently.

I smiled at him. "Go ahead. You're part of this team too."

Jordan perked up at that. "You have a team? Are we all on it?"

"Apparently. Whether any of us like it or not, given that neither of our bosses is allowed to participate." I turned to Zeke. "Let's hear it."

"There's a teacher at the supe school. Bartholomew Innes. Tholo. I was just speaking with him on another matter this morning. He might be a good resource for you for a couple of reasons. First, he's made an extensive study of the relative time differentials between realms."

"Is that why you were talking to him?" Eleri asked.

"No." He adjusted his glasses, the vision spell glinting red in the office lighting. "He had an unrelated question for me. But the other reason you might want to speak to him is that...well... he's a changeling."

CHAPTER
TEN

"Wow," Jordan breathed as Eleri whistled again.

I scratched my head. "A what now?"

"A changeling," Zeke said. "Surely you've heard of them?"

"Maybe?" I cursed myself for leaving my notepad upstairs. "In the early days, before the fae started to decrease in numbers, mostly before the industrial revolution, some humans insisted that their ill or physically or neurologically divergent children had to be changelings. Fae progeny substituted for their healthy human kids, who were stolen away into Faerie." I grimaced. "That led to some truly hideous behavior and cruelty on the part of the human parents and unimaginable suffering for the poor kids. Are you saying that sometimes it actually happened? The exchange, I mean?"

Zeke nodded. "Not as often as those human parents would have everyone believe. For one thing, fae reproduction isn't as relatively straightforward as human biology. Mal, for instance, never had a mother. He and his brothers were engendered via a spell cast at Arawn's orders, similar to the way demons are manifested by their progenitors. But sometimes, like in Niall's situation, one parent could be human, and the fae child is born in the usual way, regardless of which parent is fae."

"I think I'm gonna need a spreadsheet to keep this straight," I muttered.

"Most often, it's the mother who's human, as in Niall's case. In Tholo's case, however, it was his father who was human." He shrugged. "In traditional changeling lore, an exchange is always a given—a human child taken away with a fae child left in its place. But in reality, there's not always a one-to-one swap. Tholo's fae mother left him with his human father and vanished."

I frowned. "So…is he fae or human?"

Zeke smiled apologetically. "He's a changeling. Or that's the terminology the supe council used when they pulled him out of the foster system following the death of his human father. His specific fae nature isn't obvious, and I've never inquired about it." He colored blotchily. "That would be rude, since he's an acquaintance, not a client. However, I do know that he has extreme psychic sensitivity, far in excess of ordinary humans. In the old days, he'd probably have been burned as a witch. Luckily for him, he was born in the 1990s."

"Like me!" Jordan said. "Well, almost."

"Why do you think we should speak with him?"

"In addition to the time questions, which he might be able to help with, he'll have some of the same experiences that Wyn probably had, since Wyn was taken from his fae mother and possibly thrust into the human realm at some point. If nothing else, Tholo would be someone for Wyn to talk to, someone who might understand his situation. Because if you don't mind my expressing an opinion…"

"Never," I said.

"Once you find Wyn"—I was pleased he didn't say *if*—"he may have certain feelings about being reunited with a mother he never knew that are just as strong as the King's might be."

I blinked. "That's an excellent point. Could you contact him and ask if he could spare time to meet with us tomorrow? Maybe after the school day is over?"

Zeke nodded. "Of course."

"Excellent." I slumped again. "Now all we have to do is locate Wyn."

"Why not go back to the lake?" Jordan asked. "I promise not to let Doop track you." He reached down and scratched Doop's spine. "We have to work on his aim a little more, anyway. He keeps accidentally leaping into random dimensions all the time. It's super confusing for him."

"There's no point," I said. "Cerys told us nobody else was hanging out under the lake. She also said that some of her kind can travel between bodies of water."

Jordan shuddered. "I *really* need to keep Doop out of lakes and rivers, then. Imagine if he fell through one of those portals and the other side was deeper or farther from the shore." Jordan swallowed convulsively and then set his jaw. "Hugh, do you know how to swim?"

I blinked. "Uh…yes?"

"Could you…teach me?" He shuddered again. "I've gotta do it, even though I'm not crazy about the idea. Getting wet is bad enough, but everything looks so *weird* underwater."

I exchanged an amused glance with Eleri. "Jordan. That's what goggles are for."

"There's goggles?"

"Yep."

He sighed. "Guess I'd better get some then. Until Doop is fully trained, I need to be ready to help him. And until he stops jumping in water, that means I have to be ready to hop in, too."

He looked like he'd rather have his toenails pulled out one by one. But he'd do it for Doop. "We'll schedule our first lesson right after we solve this case. Deal?"

He beamed at me. "Sure thing, Hugh. Thanks!"

"Okay." I sat up straighter. "Now, first thing we have to do is —" Doop jumped to his feet, ears perked. I eyed him uneasily. "Did I say a trigger word of some kind?"

Jordan shook his head. "No. Other than the usual commands like *sit, stay, down,* which he already knew, the only words we've worked on so far are *walk, butt-sniffing,* and *Frisbee*. He only acts like this when somebody's at the door." He chuckled and laid a hand on Doop's back, which came up roughly to his waist. "At least he's not"—Doop growled low in his throat and the fur along his spine lifted—"growling."

CHAPTER
ELEVEN

After our unfortunate encounter with renegade angels and demons, not to mention necromancers and disgruntled fire mages, I wasn't about to ignore an early warning system. "Go ahead, Jordan. Release the hound."

Eleri snickered, but Jordan nodded, his face serious as he gazed down at Doop. "Find it out, Doop."

Doop streaked out of the lobby and up the stairs, Jordan racing along after him. I glanced at Eleri. "Coming?"

She waved me away. "Carry on. As the senior investigator on duty, this falls squarely on your shoulders. Far be it from me to usurp your authority. I'll stay here and protect the scones."

"But who'll protect them from you?" I retorted. Nevertheless, she had a point, so I took the stairs two at a time. There was no sign of Jordan or Doop on the first flight, and I didn't hear the clatter of hellhound toenails in the third-floor corridor, so I headed up to the top floor, my footsteps slightly out of sync with a faint rhythmic thumping.

Doop was facing the door next to the vending machines, the one spelled to behave like a Faerie portal. Jordan faced me with wide eyes. "Somebody's *knocking* at the door," he croaked. "I didn't know there was even a door on the other side. Sides. Whatever."

I hadn't known that either, but I was nominally in charge here, so I pretended a confidence I didn't entirely feel. "We'd best see who it is, then." I trusted the protective spells on the offices to keep us safe from anything truly dangerous. "Can you keep Doop from charging whatever's out there?"

"Doop." Jordan's voice held a note of command that I rarely —if ever—heard from the happy-go-lucky werewolf. "Sit. Stay." Doop obeyed immediately as the pounding on the door resumed.

I straightened my shoulders and grasped the doorknob. When I flung it open, a tall, reedy man nearly toppled into the corridor, overbalancing when his fist met nothing but air.

I steadied him with a hand on his elbow. "Easy, there."

He jerked his arm away and looked down his long, thin nose at me. "Where is she?"

I shared a mystified glance with Jordan as I took in our visitor. He was taller than me by a few inches, although not as tall as Lachlan—about the same height as Jordan, although not as sturdily built. His shoulders were narrow, his neck unusually long with a prominent Adam's apple, his colorless hair slicked back against his head. He sported a pencil-thin mustache I hadn't seen on anyone outside a 1930s drawing room comedy, a tweed jacket, white shirt, and brown bow tie that would make my friend David—who prided himself on his snazzy bow tie collection—weep at the wasted opportunity.

"Good afternoon," I said, attempting for a professional manner. "This is Quest Investigations, and I'm Hugh—"

"I know who you are," he said, his words clipped. "You're the fool who completely botched a simple surveillance assignment."

I blinked. Holy cow, was this… I'd never actually met the dryad clan chief, the client who'd hired Quest to document a dryad who was allegedly cheating on her tree, but this had to be him. "If you're referring to the tree of heaven stakeout—"

"Of course I am," he snapped. "A simple matter. But you couldn't manage it." He sniffed. "No better than I'd expect from a *human*, but your superiors should have assigned a competent underling, considering the stakes."

At Jordan's side, Doop began rumbling with an almost inaudible growl, and I couldn't say I blamed him. "If the stakes were so high, perhaps you should have given us more accurate intel."

He drew himself up, which made him seem even thinner. Must be a dryad thing. "Eleri Deilen was in that tree. I saw her walk into the woods myself."

Holy crap. I knew Eleri was there—she'd been with her "book club," a group of rebellious fellow dryads—in an entirely different tree. But I'd never realized that *she* was this guy's target. I mean, she complained about him enough, but—

"Nobody was in that tree," Jordan piped up. "I was there, and I"—he cut a glance at me—"know that for a fact."

The guy—what was his name? It had been in the case file. Oh, right. Coutts. Illiam Coutts. "Mr. Coutts, as was stated in our report, the tree of heaven in question was not inhabited by any supernatural entity. Whatever you suspected Eleri of doing—"

"Suspected? I know without question that she's threatening our privacy, our security, our very existence!" Jeez, he could give Athaniel, the drama queen angel, a run for his money. "I countenance her association with this...this *organization*"—he made it sound like Quest was on par with a snuff porn operation—"solely because of the rank and status of Prince Niall and Lord Maldwyn. But apparently she wastes this opportunity to advance our causes and consorts with *humans* instead."

"Now wait a minute." I was starting to get a little annoyed with this guy. "I've been vetted by the supe council—"

"Not *you*, although you're bad enough. But she was in company with a *multitude* of humans this morning, with amorous intent, in a *public place*." He sounded as shocked as any ten Victorian aunties.

"She was at the zoo with a group of friends, including several children. I hardly think—"

"Exactly! At this time of year, she should be in Faerie with all proper, right-thinking dryads, preparing for the dormant season and reflecting on her transgressions."

I almost rolled my eyes. If *that* was what Eleri was trying to avoid, I didn't blame her. "I don't think Eleri is the only dryad to choose to remain in the Outer World during the coming season. Portland winters are mild enough that—"

He jabbed his knobby finger at my face. "You tell her that I expect her in her place, comporting herself with proper contrition, by Samhain. If she flouts my authority again..." An odd expression crossed his face and I heard a distinctive *tinkle tinkle plop*.

Sure enough, when I glanced down, Doop had lifted his leg and was peeing on Coutts's brown loafers. I had no idea how the giant dog had moved so stealthily, and when I glanced at Jordan, he wore the world's fakest innocent expression.

Good dog, Doop.

"I'll be sure to give her the message. Now, if you don't mind, we have an appointment."

"But it— My shoes— The *outrage*—" he spluttered, but backed away, shaking off his shoes as Doop advanced on him with a gleam—and I mean *gleam*, as in a glow that cast shadows on the walls—in his eyes.

"Think of it as superlative fertilizer," I said as I grabbed the door. "We're thinking of marketing it. I'll give Eleri your message." I shut the door in his face and whirled to lean against it. "Whew!"

"Man," Jordan said, Doop once more sitting at his side as if he hadn't just watered the roots of the dryad clan chief, "and I thought my old pack alpha was a jerk."

I lifted an eyebrow. "Did you *encourage* Doop to take a piss on old Coutts's leg?"

"Of course not!" Jordan's mock outrage was belied by his grin. "That was Doop's idea." He shrugged. "Dryads still smell mostly like trees to him."

"You didn't stop him though."

"No." An uncharacteristic scowl marred Jordan's good-natured face. "That man wasn't very nice. Not to you. Not to Eleri. And he never even *looked* at Doop and me, as though we weren't even worth his notice. I mean, *hello*? Hellhound? Doop at least deserves the respect of acknowledgement."

"I don't know. Wouldn't eye contact be seen as a threat or a dominance challenge?"

"Then he should learn the best way to greet a dog as an equal."

I checked out the floor. The puddle wasn't as large as I'd expect from a dog Doop's size—most of it was probably still soaking Coutts's pant leg and puddling inside his shoes—but it wasn't insignificant. "You know, Jordan, I don't think you should leave that for Zeke to clean up. He'd probably do it because he's Zeke, but—"

"Oh, no worries," he said brightly. "I intended to clean it, anyway. I've got the supplies in my backpack downstairs."

"I suppose we'd better give Eleri her message." I headed for the stairs.

"She won't have to leave Quest all winter, will she?" Jordan and Doop pattered down the steps at my side.

"Not if I have anything to say about it," I muttered. "I'm sure Niall will intercede with the King." Assuming Niall wasn't still in a royal snit about Cerys come Samhain.

After a quick stop to retrieve my notepad, we clattered on down into the lobby. Jordan headed directly for the backpack, which was leaning against the wall behind Zeke's desk.

I glanced around the office, but Eleri was alone. "Where's Zeke?"

"He left for that Hunter's Moon rehearsal. I think hearts might have actually been floating over his head at the notion."

She grinned over the rim of her tea cup. "Doop looks in better spirits. Canine crisis averted?"

"Yes," Jordan said, rummaging in the pack. "He peed on Mr. Coutts's feet and made him leave, so everything's fine."

She choked on her tea, spraying it onto her denim skirt and floral leggings. "Illiam was here?"

I nodded. "He heard about your zoo excursion and chose to take exception to your companions."

"How did he— Schefflera." She scowled. "They're all over the place and they're the *worst* gossips. Doop watered his shoes?"

"Yep." Jordan held up a huge spray bottle of greenish liquid. "But don't worry. I'll clean it up. Bryce made this stuff *especially* for hellhound...accidents."

"You called him a hellhound upstairs too." I took a seat next to Eleri. "I thought we weren't allowed to call him that because of positive reinforcement?"

"It *is* positive reinforcement if it's said with love. And when he does hellhound-type stuff for good reasons."

Eleri chuckled. "Good boy, Doop. Keep up the superlative work." She gaped as Jordan pulled a bundle of rags out of his pack. "Oak and thorn, Jordan, what else do you have in there?"

"Oh, different stuff," he said absently as he struggled with a stubborn zipper. "Treats, toys, brushes, a toenail clipper, antibiotics, pooper bags, bandages, a couple of Frisbees. You know, just the essentials."

Eleri smirked at me. "Parents of toddlers carry diaper bags. Jordan carries—"

"Don't say it." I pinched the bridge of my nose.

"—a Dooper bag."

"Brother," I muttered. "If you're resorting to comments like that, we need to take a hard left and get back to the case." I balanced a notepad on my knee. "First thing we need to do is find Wyn, but in order to do that, we need to contact Herne."

"That would make finding Wyn the second thing," Eleri said.

"Don't split hairs." I tapped my pad. "The problem is that Herne's horn is back in the forge now, and from what Mal said, Govannon isn't taking any chances with it. Nor is Herne. He almost didn't want to let it go after he got it back from Melchom and Athaniel, except his mandate specifies that there has to be some way for people to summon him at need." I thought about that, about Herne's compulsion to answer the call of the horn, about Cerys's enforced separation from children and abusive partners, about Grizel's obligation to answer three questions of anybody who kept her from reaching the safety of her stream.

Man, the elder gods had a *real* problem with consent.

Jordan stood up, his arms full of cleaning supplies. "If you want to talk to Herne, why not just text him?"

Eleri and I both did a slow pan to gape at him. "I'm sorry," I said. "What now?"

Jordan cocked one hip in a way that was probably meant to indicate the cell phone in his pocket. "Text Herne. Ask him to meet us in Faerie."

"Okay." I pinched the bridge of my nose again. Jeez, I was turning into Niall. "First, Herne has a cell phone?"

Jordan scoffed. "Well, *obviously*. How else could he get catfished on that fake dating app by the sleazy angel guy?"

"The kid's got a point," Eleri said. "Although I admit it never occurred to me. That doesn't explain why *you* have his number, though."

Pink infused Jordan's cheeks. "I, um, had questions. About Doop and his care." He glared at us. "It's *important*, okay? I didn't want him to get sick, but no way was I on board with that whole flesh of traitors food source thing. After the first couple of times we kinda surprised Herne by showing up on his doorstep —well, at his hollow tree—he gave me his number."

"How did you find this...hollow tree?" I asked faintly. I prided myself a little on applying human logic and problem-solving in dealing with the supernatural community and its restrictions, but Jordan managed to get results by ignoring the restrictions completely. Or else being sublimely unaware of them. Maybe the real strategy for circumventing supe rules and traditions was just to plow right through the middle of them.

"Oh, *I* couldn't." He beamed down at Doop, who gazed up at him in adoration. "That was all Doop. He can always find Herne. Just like he can always find me, whether I'm wolfy or humanish. It's everything *else* we have to work on. Like knowing who to pee on."

"Well, I think he's got that part down," I muttered. "Do you think you could text Herne for us, please?"

"Oh, sure!" He lifted his supplies. "As soon as I clean up Doop's…stuff. After all, taking care of him is my job."

He bustled out of the room, Doop at his heels.

CHAPTER TWELVE

Jordan was as good as his word. Not only were the fourth-floor corridor tiles sparkling clean and smelling of lemon and eucalyptus instead of hellhound pee, but standing on the other side of the portal at the edge of a Faerie meadow was a six and a half foot tall guy with a twenty-four point rack of antlers on his head and the full pack of *Cwn Annwn* at his back.

Herne the Hunter.

I recognized his outfit. It was the same—or at least identical—to the clothes we rescued from Grizel's laundry of doom in our last case, except he'd added a gray, silk-lined cape. I hoped Edna Mode's dire warnings about *No capes!* weren't about to bite Herne on the ass.

He inclined his head. "Hugh. I am pleased to see you."

"Um, me too," I croaked. Herne was that kind of guy, if you know what I mean? Imposing, even if after our little adventure in Sheol, I didn't find him intimidating. Well, not much. "Thank you for coming."

He smiled, and when he wasn't either starving or in battle mode, his expressions could be quite sweet. "Of course. You may call on me at any time."

I studied his rack. It wouldn't fit through our door, and although I knew he could shed it at will and grow it back when he rode on the Hunt, I didn't want to ask it of him. He'd only just grown it back when he'd chased down and, er, *dispatched*

Melchom and Athaniel for their role in his own kidnapping and the death of the old kennel master.

I was *so* glad I didn't know the details of that little escapade. *The flesh of traitors.* I eyed the hounds. They were all sitting, alert, their attention focused on Herne as though waiting for his signal to...do something. The difference between their almost palpable edge of menace and Doop's puppyish innocence was remarkable. I hoped Doop would never lose his goofy friendliness and turn into that kind of weapon.

I could only hope that the pack's behavior was the result of nurture, not nature, and that Doop being socialized by Jordan and his Dog House pack mates would make the difference. Jordan had declined to stay and greet Herne, explaining that the other *Cwn Annwn* made Doop nervous, and that he may have inadvertently caused a problem for Herne by introducing the other hounds to Frisbee.

"I'd ask you to join us here, but"—I gestured to Herne's antlers—"you might be more comfortable on that side of the portal."

"I reside not in Faerie, so one place is as good as another." He smiled again. "And I have grown adept at traversing doors of late. After our shared adventure, and given that architecture has changed markedly from when I coursed often in the Outer World, I deemed it prudent to consult with several adepts in configuring a spell to make doorways accommodate my person. Now, I have only to ask." He spoke a few words in a low voice —I suspected they were Welsh or Gaelic. Not English, in any case. And when he stepped forward, the doorway... accommodated him.

Wow. That must be something like the way Eleri could ask the trees to move when she whispered to them. Maybe supes of all natures were learning about consent. Although...

"Are doorways allowed to refuse you?"

He glanced around the hallway, and I noted that although the door adapted, the ceiling of our corridor? Not so much. The tips of his antlers grazed the acoustic tiles, causing flecks of white to patter down onto the floor. I made a mental note to speak to Zeke about it—if Herne was going to be a regular visitor, we'd either need to adjust Quest's building spells or add a budget line item for ceiling repair. At least our landlord was a supe—a swan shifter who was also a financial whiz—so the request wouldn't be refused outright.

"If the folk on the other side of the door do not wish me to enter, and they are not my rightful prey, I must await their pleasure."

"They have to invite you in?" Casimir told me the old myth about inviting vampires to cross your threshold was garbage, but apparently the restriction still held for horned meta-gods who tracked down traitors for a living.

"As you say."

I eyed the pack, still waiting on the other side of the portal. "Um, I don't think we have room for the hounds."

"Of course not." He turned and made a swift gesture with one hand. The hounds immediately stood and raced off across the meadow until they disappeared beyond a hill. "They need time to bond with the new kennel master in any case."

"This way, please." I led him down the stairs to the Little Conference Room. The ceiling in here was higher—don't ask me how that worked. Our building had definite quirks, which is why asking for higher ceilings in the hallways wasn't as outlandish as you might think. Maybe the ceilings could be enlarged into an alternate dimension, the way St. Stupid's added wards and storage space when they needed extra capacity.

I had expected Eleri to be awaiting us, along with any scones that escaped her predations, while Jordan manned the phones in Zeke's absence. What I hadn't expected, however, was Lachlan, looming next to the windows with his arms crossed and an expression like a storm at sea.

I may have mentioned once or twice that Lachlan can be a grumpy cuss at the best of times. But I'd never seen him looking quite so…thunderous. Scratch that—I had, but it was back when I'd first met him, and he'd been facing down hostile opponents, including one of my bosses.

I decided to ignore the stroppy selkie for the moment and play host. "Herne, this is Eleri Deilen, another Quest junior investigator." Eleri's eyes widened at that, but she shook off her shock with a delighted grin. "She wasn't with us in Sheol."

His brow wrinkled as though he were considering a knotty problem. "A visit to Sheol would be quite chancy for a dryad." He eyed Lachlan, who was still doing his angry Haystack Rock impression. "For a selkie too, methinks."

Lachlan just grunted. Eleri, bless her, leaped into the breach. "Exactly," she said. "May I offer you something to eat? Drink?"

Herne hesitated, but only for a moment. "Thank you. That would be welcome. I must remember that this place isn't like Faerie of old, nor like Hades, where partaking of food or drink will tie one to the realm for eternity."

I blinked. "Ah. No. The Quest offices are a safe space, even for sharing true names. If you would excuse me for a moment, I need to confer with…my colleague." I glared at Lachlan and jerked my head toward the door. "Outside."

I strode to the door, not bothering to check to see if Lachlan was following, Eleri's overbright chatter to Herne a counterpoint to my footsteps. I moved down the hallway until I passed the first curve—yeah, curved halls in a rectilinear building. Like I said, the place had its quirks.

I turned to face him. "What's the deal? Why are you so mad at me?"

His jaw actually dropped in the most ridiculous expression of shock. Then he scrubbed both hands over his face and sighed. "I'm not angry with you, Matthew." He rested one of his big hands on my shoulder with surprising gentleness. "I could never be angry with you."

I lifted an eyebrow. "I'd suggest you not make any rash promises. You haven't known me that long."

His eyes glinted when he smiled. "Long enough."

Before I could get lost in that smile and lose my common sense, I stepped back out of reach and his hand dropped to his side. "If you're not mad at me, then what's going on? We've got a case to solve, and if you somehow missed it"—I jabbed my finger in the direction of the conference room—"we've got Herne on the premises. We can't waste time or opportunity because you're in a bad mood."

"I know. It's just..." He sighed again, and something like sadness flickered across his broad face. "Blair's sorry excuse for a father. He took Blair to task for our little trip today." He winced. "Apparently they hadn't exactly received permission."

I frowned. "That's usually a yes-no question. Did they receive permission or not?" A big man like Lachlan taking a child away from their home without a parent's knowledge or consent was an Amber alert waiting to happen.

"They weren't *forbidden* to go, and given that wanker's usual neglect of the poor mite, Blair took it as tacit agreement." He carded his hands through his hair. "I stepped in and took the brunt of Floyd's temper, but I'm worried Blair's in for a miserable time of it."

My belly clenched. "He wouldn't... I mean, he doesn't *hurt* Blair, does he?"

Lachlan's mouth twisted with disgust. "Define *hurt*. If you mean, does he strike them, no." The prodigious scowl was back. "If I'd ever had the least inkling that he had, I'd have contacted child protective services in a heartbeat, regardless of what Blair wishes. But words can hurt too. Inconsistent reactions to ordinary things, like today's trip. When you can't depend on someone, someone who has power over you, to behave in a predictable way, then you'll never feel truly safe."

I shifted uneasily. I was worried for Blair, yes. They were vulnerable in so many ways. But I worried about Lachlan, too.

Wyn had certainly behaved in unpredictable ways in the past, and though some of it wasn't his fault—being magically roofied by an unscrupulous mage for the benefit of his loser son a case in point—he'd definitely done a number on Lachlan.

But if I had my way, and if Herne came through for us, that toxic connection was about to be cut for good, both literally—when their handfasting knot was severed—and figuratively, when Lachlan finally stopped feeling responsible for Wyn's happiness.

I gave myself a mental facepalm. Who was I kidding? Lachlan's protective streak was a mile wide. He'd *always* feel responsible for Wyn's happiness, just as he felt responsible for Blair's, and, it seemed, was coming to feel for mine. The problem was that he was so incredibly strong-willed and stubborn that his notion of what constituted happiness for anyone didn't necessarily jibe with theirs.

Take the selkie clans, for instance. They wanted their king to take the throne and rule. Lachlan thought they'd be better off— *happier*—learning to govern themselves more democratically.

But if Lachlan felt responsible for my happiness, I felt just as responsible for his. Confronting Wyn again was going to be painful for him, bringing past hurts and betrayals back to light, but there was no way to dodge it, not for any of our sakes.

I stepped toward him again and laced our fingers together. "I'd say you don't need to stay, but it's not true. If Herne is able to determine Wyn's location, you'll need to be there too, so he feels safe. He's only met me once for about three minutes—and they weren't my finest minutes either. Herne is enough to scare the pants off anyone, and the last time he saw Eleri, she was more or less the gatekeeper for his roofier. I hate to ask—"

"I'll be there," he said, tightening his fingers. "You shouldn't have to ask, and I'm sorry that you do. I'll check on Blair after a bit." He snorted. "Floyd wouldn't let me past their door now, anyway."

I smiled up at him. "Talk to Herne. He might be able to help with getting past doors." At Lachlan's quizzical look, I squeezed his hands once and let go. "Never mind. We've got a meta-god to petition. Coming?"

At his nod, I led the way back to the conference room. Herne was seated at the head of the table, his antlers back-lit impressively by the windows. He was calmly eating a poppyseed scone as Eleri set a glass of iced tea next to his plate. She looked a little white around the eyes, but Herne was a big part of her personal cultural footprint, just as Govannon was, so I expect she was freaking out a little.

I took my place at his right while Lachlan sat across from me on his left. I cleared my throat. "I wanted to thank you for the information you shared with Lachlan about Wyn's whereabouts after your return from Sheol."

He nodded regally. "It was the least I could do after your signal service to me and mine."

"Yes. Well." I cleared my throat again and smiled at Eleri gratefully when she handed me a bottle of water. I took a swig. "The thing is, by the time we were able to follow up, Wyn had already moved on."

Herne's brows drew together. "Moved on? Where?"

"That, er, was what we were hoping you could tell us."

He glanced at Lachlan. "You did not move with sufficient dispatch?"

"It wasn't his fault," I said quickly. "The beaver clan who owns the lake wouldn't allow access until this morning because of their own lake activities."

"Ah," he said. "I understand." He wiped his fingers fastidiously with one of Zeke's linen napkins—he objected to paper napkins on principle, a principle firmly supported by Eleri—and stood up. "Then let us go."

I gaped up at him, towering over us like a giant animated coatrack. "Go?"

"Yes." He gazed at each of us in turn. "If the target is on the move, then providing you with his current fixed location will not be helpful. He could have moved again by the time you're able to travel there by your inefficient Outer World transportation methods."

"We, ah, can use the FTA. But unless Wyn is someplace secluded, someplace out of human view, we won't be able to exit." Humans tended to take exception to people appearing out of thin air.

He gave us an almost pitying look. "I do not travel through Faerie. I travel on the night."

On the night? I shared a mystified glance with Eleri. "What exactly does that mean?"

He shrugged his massive shoulders. "Where the night is, there am I. If I name you as my companions, you may accompany me, much as my hounds do when the Wild Hunt rides."

I wasn't entirely sure I liked being put on the same level as a dog, but there were certainly worse things. According to much of the supe community, *human* was one of those worse things, but lately I'd started to believe that wasn't the case at all.

We humans had our own magic—adaptability and ingenuity, not to mention freedom from the paranormal rules that bound so many supes. Which, let me tell you, could come in *extremely* handy.

I glanced at the window. Daylight had begun to fade, so if *night* was the requirement for this little jaunt, we were close. My veins *zing*ed with excitement.

Almost. This case was almost solved—all I needed to do was introduce Wyn to Cerys. I didn't even need to wait for our appointment. I could do it tonight, as soon as Herne led us to him.

Then, not only would my first solo case be a success, but Lachlan would be free. Or at least *nearly* free. He and Wyn still needed to stand before the King at their sundering ceremony and have their knot severed. I winced. Would the King have second thoughts about allowing the sundering once he found out Wyn was his half-brother, either because he wanted to protect him, or because he wanted vengeance?

I shook that thought off. From everything I knew about the King, he wasn't vindictive. Niall, on the other hand... I really hoped Niall didn't find some reason to prevent the ceremony, just to spite Cerys, especially since he was about to tie his own knot with Gareth.

Oh well. I'd worry about that when the time came. For now, we needed to travel on the night.

CHAPTER THIRTEEN

"Where's the best place to, er, launch?" I asked Herne as we gathered in the fourth floor corridor. Our little group included me, Lachlan, and Eleri, but not Jordan or Doop. Jordan had promised to man the office for Zeke, so he volunteered—mournfully, and with the air of somebody about to be burned at the stake—to stay behind, determined to prove his reliability.

Herne glanced around, taking in the vending machines and the portal door. And in case you're wondering? We all kept a very healthy distance from him, so his antlers didn't take out an eye when he turned his head. "Any place open to the night will do. This passageway will not, since it has no windows and no moving air. We could cross into Faerie. Or we could return to the room we just left and open a window."

I thought about that for a minute. Clearly, *traveling on the night* wasn't going to be as simple as hiking down to the nearest MAX stop and buying a ticket. And though Portlanders were serious about their commitment to keeping the city weird, I didn't really think Herne would pass unremarked—or worse, unrecorded. That guy on the unicycle wearing a kilt and Darth Vader mask while playing flaming bagpipes was still getting YouTube hits, and Herne was right up there with him on the weirdness scale, even without the cape.

"Do you actually know where Wyn is?"

He regarded me somberly. "Not yet."

"Then maybe we should stick with Faerie. You might cause a bit of a stir on the sidewalks, even after dark."

He smiled rather grimly—and before you ask, it was only his antlers that were deer-like. His face and (as far as I could tell from the way he filled out his jerkin) body were pretty standard high fae issue: built and beautiful, not necessarily in that order.

Not that I was looking for anything other than professional observational purposes. Not when Lachlan was standing right next to me in all his grumpy beefcake glory.

"When I hunt," Herne said, "none perceive my pursuit. Not unless I will it."

Okay. Good to know. Niall had mentioned that Herne's quarry couldn't detect him when he hunted, but I didn't realize that his cloak of invisibility extended to random hangers-on. After all, *we* could see him. Of course, he wasn't hunting at the moment, and he was probably *willing* us to see him. I made a mental note to add this little factlet to my Herne dossier.

However, I had serious doubts about my own ability to herd a possibly undetectable supernatural hunter, a dryad BFF, and a boyfriend-to-be on a search that had no defined endpoint.

"Do you suppose you could be a little more specific about where we'll end up?" I patted my camera bag. "I mean, we had to make some significant equipment upgrades before we hit Govannon's forge, not to mention Sheol."

He waved my words away. "While you hunt with me, you shall be under my mantle. Have no fear."

I narrowed my eyes. Considering I'd met Herne the first time after he'd been trapped in Sheol for days, I wasn't sure how confident I was with these vague assurances. But what choice did we have? If we wanted to find Wyn, Herne was our only shot. Unless I wanted to trust Doop's tracking ability, and I wasn't sure I'd *ever* be there, despite Jordan's unquenchable optimism.

Apparently, we weren't going to get any more pre-launch intel from Herne, so I sighed and keyed in the portal code for Faerie.

We arrived at the foot of the tor. Somewhere in the dense woods on its crown was the ceilidh glade, the Stone Circle, and beyond that, the kennels. The Keep, where the King and Queen lived and held court, was in a completely different spot, although Eleri always claimed that Faerie geography wasn't fixed, and could choose to be helpful, neutral, or downright antagonistic. Luckily, we didn't have to assess its current mood, because if it took its cues from its royalty, it might be feeling a tad vindictive this evening.

"Would each of you take hold of my cloak?" He gazed down —or in Lachlan's case, across—at each of us. "Do not release it until I give you leave, else you will suffer the consequences."

"Well, *that's* not ominous," I muttered as I gripped a fistful of Herne's cape. It was turning into my mantra.

Eleri and Lachlan followed suit, Lachlan lacing the fingers of our free hands together, and I felt like a low-rent version of the bridal minions who wrangled Princess Diana's twenty-five-foot wedding train, even though Herne's cape only hit him mid-thigh. But they were really long thighs, okay? Kind of in proportion to the rest of him. He glanced over his shoulder, as if to check that we'd followed orders, and then lifted his chin, eyes halfway closed, nostrils flaring.

Searching. Did he use scent? Sound? Good vibrations? He was a supe, for Pete's sake. A supe who *traveled on the night*, and hunted down criminals, with a full mandate to execute them when he caught them. Considering how cryptic Herne was at the best of times—and unnervingly direct at others, like when he vowed vengeance for the former kennel master's death—he probably couldn't tell me how he did it even if I got up the gumption to ask.

Before I could get even more up in my head about the strangeness, we were suddenly...moving. But not moving?

More like we were standing still and everything else was whirling past us: woods, meadows, mountains, rivers, houses, highways, deserts, sky, stars—heck, were those *planets*? Was that *lava*? And suddenly I figured it out: earth, water, air, fire. The elements answered to him—or maybe he answered to them.

It hardly mattered which, but I tightened my grip on Herne's cape. I was probably punching holes in the silk and velvet with my fingernails, even though I couldn't feel it any more than I could feel Lachlan's hand in mine.

Then, as suddenly as we were moving, we weren't. There was no thump, no shock, no stumbling. We were simply still, in the midst of more stillness.

I blinked at our surroundings. We were in a good-sized room —roughly the footprint of my tiny rental house—with a rustic cabin feel. There was a cheery though not roaring fire in the stone fireplace, the flames reflecting on the polished wood floor and casting dancing shadows on several rag rugs. A small kitchen with a two-burner stove, a soapstone sink, and a dorm-sized fridge was tucked in one corner. A drop-leaf table and two chairs sat in front of it, opposite a sofa and easy chair upholstered in a blue and green tartan.

"Clan Urquhart," Lachlan murmured, trailing a finger along the chair's back. "Hmmm."

Tartan curtains—apparently Clan Urquhart—covered the windows, and candles flickered on the mantelpiece and the oak-plank coffee table.

I peered around more closely as Eleri wandered over to a window, Lachlan poked at the fire, and Herne loomed in the corner.

Other than a six-panel door, partially ajar, next to the fireplace, there were no other entrances or exits. I itched to explore, if only to figure out where the heck we were.

"Uh...Hugh?" Eleri was staring outside, her hands clutching the parted curtains.

"Yeah?"

"Could you come here, please?"

I frowned, because Eleri never sounded that... discombobulated. She was pretty much the definition of *shut up and deal*. So I hurried over to stand next to her. "What is—*whoa!*" A school of silvery fish darted past the window. "That's no forest."

I'd have expected Eleri to bite back with a snide remark, but she just continued to stare outside into the oddly illuminated water. An instant later, the illumination was explained—more or less—when a sinuous, iridescent purple scaled tail undulated past the glass. The light seemed to be coming *from* the scales.

Then the tail whipped around and I had to clutch the window sill, hoping really, really hard that the glass was indestructible, because *yikes!* "I've never seen a sea serpent with *eyelashes* before."

"Exactly how many sea serpents *have* you seen, Hugh?"

"Well. None. But I never *imagined* eyelashes on any of them." Then it struck me. "Holy crap. Is that the Loch Ness *Monster*?" My voice squeaked on the last word.

"Loch Ness is part of Clan Urquhart's hereditary lands," Lachlan said with a nod at the plaid furniture, "although I doubt yon lady considers herself so monstrous as all that."

"Right. Sorry. But that means we're at the at the bottom of a freaking *loch*." I glanced at the fridge, where it hummed nonchalantly under the kitchen counter. "How do they get electricity down here?"

"I don't care about electricity," Eleri wailed. "How did *we* get down here?"

"On the night," Herne rumbled.

She pointed at the window. "Is it night now? How can you tell? What if it's noon up above the water?"

He regarded her, unperturbed. "It is night somewhere."

"Fabulous," she muttered, frowning. "I feel so much better." There was a gasp behind us and we whirled.

Wyn, his eyes huge in his pale face, was standing inside the doorway, a quilt-covered bed behind him. From where he stood, he could only see me, Eleri, and Herne—Lachlan was still out of his sightline by the fireplace. He wasn't wearing the trendy red coat he'd sported when I'd seen him last, and in contrast to Herne, his narrow gray trousers and pale blue button-down were more Fashion Week than Ren Faire. He clutched the door, mouth working.

I raised one hand in greeting. "Hi, Wyn. We've been looking for you."

He slammed the door and a moment later, a deadbolt clicked. And another. And a third.

I shared a rueful glance with Eleri. "That went well." I grimaced at the *very* closed door. "Although why would anyone need three locks on a door under a freaking *loch*?"

"We don't know this is a loch," Eleri said.

"It is," Herne stated. "Hugh is correct. Loch Ness."

"But why would Wyn hide—" I slapped my forehead. "D'oh! The last time he saw me was in Pierce Martinson's creepy study when I was questioning him about tossing dead fish at Lachlan's boat."

She winced. "And I was the Martinson's maid. He probably thinks we're here on the Martinsons' behalf. To take him back to them. He doesn't know they're no threat anymore." She glanced at Herne. "Herne's presence probably isn't exactly comforting either, considering the whole death-to-traitors thing."

"But Wyn's not a traitor," I said. She cut a glance at Lachlan. "Oh. Right. *That* kind of betrayal."

"I'll talk to him." Lachlan set aside the fireplace poker and moved to the door. Since Lachlan had enabled Wyn's disappearing act, surely he'd know he could trust Lachlan now. So why hadn't Lachlan stepped in when Wyn first appeared?

Then I considered *Lachlan's* perspective. His expression was hard to read. Was that regret? Sorrow? Determination? He'd cared enough about Wyn at one point to marry him, and later, to help him escape the Martinsons. Facing Wyn again with that baggage between them couldn't be easy.

He paused, his fist raised to knock on the door, and looked back at me. I gave him what I hoped was a reassuring smile and a nod. His shoulders dropped from where they'd been bunched around his ears, so I guess I was successful. More or less.

"Wyn?" he called softly. "It's all right, *mo ghràidh*. You've nothing to fear. Not from us, and not from the Martinsons."

No sound at first, but then each of the locks clicked and Wyn peered out the cracked door. "Lachlan? What are you doing here?"

CHAPTER
FOURTEEN

Lachlan's smile was a little forced. "We've come to let you know you've no reason to hide any longer. Everyone here is a friend."

The sliver of Wyn's face I could see telegraphed his skepticism. "Lachlan," he hissed, "that's *Herne the Hunter* over there. Not to mention the Martinson's maid, and that human from the investigation firm. How could they possibly be *friends*?" Now that telegraphed look was loaded with hurt and betrayal. "You *promised*. You promised you wouldn't tell."

"Ah, well. Things have changed a wee bit."

"What things?" Suspicion was clear in Wyn's tone.

Rather than leaving Lachlan twisting in the wind, I stepped forward. "Both Martinsons have been apprehended for illegal magical activity—including the coercive spells they placed on you—and sentenced to hard labor in Govannon's forge."

Eleri appeared at my shoulder. "I'm sorry I didn't help you sooner. I couldn't enter Pierce's workroom without getting singed, so I didn't know what he was doing at first." She spread her arms. "I expect that's why he hired a dryad in the first place —to keep *the help* out of his business."

Wyn continued to regard us out of his one visible eye. "So why is *he* here?"

Obviously he meant Herne. "We needed his help to find you," I said. "So we could ask you to return and handle a little unfinished business. Your own and others'." I didn't want to bring Cerys into this yet. I might be sure Wyn was her missing child, but that didn't mean he was anxious to meet her—Niall's reaction had given me severe doubts about the success of this little family reunion.

"Wyn." Lachlan's voice was soft, cajoling. Did a shard of jealousy stab me in the middle, wondering whether Lachlan sounded like that when he was inviting Wyn into bed? I'd like to say it was beneath me, that their past relationship was none of my business. But what can I say? I'm human, dammit.

However, it was their future relationship—specifically, the end of it—that truly concerned me. Besides, bringing Wyn in to meet Cerys was how to solve my case. If Lachlan was the one he trusted, then I could bite down on my unreasonable jealousy and deal.

Mostly.

Lachlan extended one big, broad hand. "Won't you come out? Matthew has some questions for you." He cut a glance at me. "As do I."

"I… I'm not sure I'm ready." Wyn's voice was barely audible. "Even if, as you say, the Martinsons are contained—"

"No harm will come to you," Herne rumbled. "You are out of time."

I frowned at Herne. "He's not out of time. There's no specific deadline. I admit we'd like to move things along, but—"

"Lad," Lachlan said, a smile buried in his tone, "Herne meant that we're *outside* of time, not that time is running out."

I blinked. "You're kidding." Crap, I really wanted to take notes on this. "You mean time isn't passing here?" I glared at him. "And stop calling me *lad*."

To his credit, Lachlan winced. "Sorry, la— Matthew. I'll try to remember." He glanced at Herne. "I'm right, am I not, that this little bubble is like Faerie, running at its own pace?" Herne nodded, and Lachlan turned to me. "So while time isn't standing still—"

"Or running backward," Eleri said.

"—there's no reason to rush."

I forced myself to take a deep, steady breath. I didn't want to hang out here for some unspecified amount of alternate time while Wyn decided whether he wanted to come out and talk to us. But I also wasn't an asshole like Reid Martinson, who coerced him into betraying Lachlan and—

Crap. Now that Wyn *wasn't* coerced, maybe his reasons for severing the knot were gone, too. I gripped my camera bag strap and took *another* deep breath. I'd learned patience the hard way—hunting for the perfect cryptid photo op, waiting for Ted to notice me, staking out freaking *trees* for Quest. Surely I could be patient now and trust that Lachlan truly wanted to be with me the way he'd said.

He was a selkie. He'd sworn on the heart of the sea, so he'd keep his promise to me.

But hadn't he made promises to Wyn first? Which one would win out in the end?

I resigned myself to a few non-hours of waiting, but Wyn surprised me.

He laughed, a soft chuckle that was a little too appealing for my liking, and glanced from me to Lachlan. "So *that's* why you're in a hurry."

Lachlan flushed above his close-trimmed beard and stared at the floor. Wait. Lachlan was *blushing*. He was embarrassed? "Not altogether."

Wyn opened the door and stood framed there, perfectly lit from a source I couldn't detect. "We didn't really meet properly last time." He held out his hand to me. "Wyn Ellis. Lachlan is a good man. You're very lucky."

"Uh…" I glanced at Eleri, who shrugged, so I gulped and shook Wyn's hand. It was pale, long-fingered, soft, and completely opposite my square, callused paws. "Thanks?"

When I'd met him that day at the Martinsons, I'd been struck by his beauty—his delicate features, his ethereal grace. But now

I could trace the resemblance between him and Cerys: the high cheekbones, the short, straight nose, the peat-brown hair. Oh, yeah. Unless all Welsh water fae shared the same genetics, he was definitely her kid.

Now all I had to do was convince him to come back to Quest to meet her.

From the corner, Herne sucked in a hissing breath, his eyes burning—literally—as he stared at Wyn. "You're more beautiful than the angel." He made it sound like an accusation, not a compliment.

Apparently, I wasn't the only one who thought so, because Wyn ducked back into the bedroom and slammed the door.

I glared at Herne. "Thanks a lot." When Eleri laughed, I glared at her, too. "You're no help."

"Oh, come on, Hugh. Don't you get it? Herne didn't say *an* angel, he said *the* angel. Athaniel. The one who catfished him with that fake dating app."

I lifted my eyebrows. "Seriously?" When I glanced at Herne, he shuffled uncomfortably and then turned to face the wall. "We can still see you, you know."

"I beg your pardon," he mumbled. "I meant no disrespect."

I sighed. "Dude. No wonder you can't get a date. You really need to up your game." I turned to Lachlan. "Do you think you could sweet-talk Wyn into joining us out here if you let him know Herne doesn't mean any harm, he just has really awkward pickup lines?"

Lachlan huffed a laugh. "I'll try." He knocked softly on the door. "Wyn? May I come in?" I heard something muffled from inside the room, but it must have been an invitation, because Lachlan slipped inside.

"Guess we wait," Eleri said as she strolled over to the kitchen. She lifted the kettle from the stove and swished it, judging its contents. "Anyone want tea?"

"No, thanks." I checked on Herne, who was still standing in the corner like a toddler in time out. "If you can find anything stronger, Herne looks like he could use a drink."

So could I, for that matter. I was under *Loch Ness*, for Pete's sake, and—*awp!* There was an enormous emerald eye staring in the window. That was *Nessie*. A shot of her would have scored me *millions* if I'd still been hawking cryptid photos to the tabloids. Now I just wanted to photograph her because she was beautiful.

I slowly lowered my bag to the table, but as soon as I lifted the camera out, the eye disappeared. *Dammit.* I hesitated for a moment before I switched out my 50mm lens for the telephoto that I'd gotten at Stuff 'n' Things. It had revealed a little too much when I'd used it in Sheol—invisible souls, for one thing— but it had also helped me rescue Herne. I hoped there weren't any invisible beings hanging around in here, because I wasn't sure I was ready for this visit to get even more bizarre. But just in case, I'd keep the camera pointed safely out the window, thanks.

Pushing the curtains all the way aside, I looked out and breathed a sigh of relief and wonder, almost light-headed because Nessie hadn't left altogether. She was still out there, cutting sinuous figure-eights through the surprisingly clear water. I lifted my camera and activated the video function. It was almost as if she could tell I was filming her, because she was showing off, practically flirting with the camera, scales glowing, occasionally peering coyly over her shoulder. A bubble of joy rose in my chest, because *this. This* was what I'd always wanted, always dreamed of from the time I was a boy. This world. This magic.

"Hugh? Are you sure you don't want any tea?" At my shoulder, Eleri held out a steaming white ceramic mug.

I nearly fumbled my camera. I hadn't heard the kettle whistle, hadn't heard her approach, hadn't heard anything while I'd watched Nessie frolic. I swung around, the lens nearly whacking Eleri in the side of the head. "Yikes! Sorry. No. Not now." I kept turning in a complete 360 so I faced the window again, but the water outside was dark and empty. Nessie was gone.

I sighed and lowered the camera, switching off the video. "Damn."

"Oh, Hugh." Eleri bit her lip. "I'm sorry. I didn't mean to—"

"No, it's okay." I smiled at her and put the camera away carefully. I'd be able to pull some stills out of the video—not to sell, but to mount in my Quest office as a reminder that no matter what happened with Lachlan and me, my life as it was now was really the best. I zipped up the bag and accepted the tea. "Thanks for this." I took a sip. "How long was I"—I gestured to the window with my mug—"zoned out?"

She grinned. "How would I know? We're out of time here, remember?"

I shook my head. "Dryad humor is the worst."

"You mean the best. Come on, admit it."

"Not a chance." I checked on Herne. He was out of the corner and huddled at the table, staring into the tea mug cradled between his hands. The size of the furniture compared to his, er, mythic stature made him look like a kindergarten teacher sitting at the kids' table. Assuming any kindergarten teacher anywhere had a twenty-four point rack on their head. "He okay?" I murmured.

She shrugged. "Moping. We really need to find him a date." She brightened. "He seemed quite taken with Wyn. Maybe—"

"I can hear you, you know," Herne muttered into his tea. "You saw him. He was revolted by me, just as the angel was."

I walked over and sat in the chair across from him, which fit me a lot better. "First, Athaniel was an asshole. Second, your comment was a little…hostile."

He lifted his chin and met my gaze, his eyes wide and not glowing at all. In fact, he looked kinda devastated. "You think I *frightened* him?" He dropped his head, and I had to rear back to keep from having an eye poked out. "I am a monster."

I sighed. "Dude." I patted his arm. "You're not a monster."

"I am," he moaned. "I am terrible. A menace. I *executed* the last person I dated."

I blinked. Okay, that wasn't exactly a glowing reference for future boyfriends. "I don't think you ever achieved date status with Athaniel. You were his victim first, and afterward, you were doing your job. Wyn's not Athaniel." I tried to keep my tone hearty and encouraging. "Besides, he's married to Lachlan, so he's used to guys with uncertain tempers."

That didn't reassure Herne as much as I'd hoped. His head dropped lower. "He's *married*?"

"Well. Not for much longer. That's one of the reasons we were trying to find him, remember?"

He peered up at me from below the thicket of antlers. "Really?"

"Absolutely. And after the sundering ceremony, maybe you could approach him. Nicely."

He heaved a huge sigh. "I have never done such a thing. I do not know how."

"Cheer up," Eleri said brightly. "We'll help."

"We will?" I asked faintly.

She shot me a narrow-eyed glance. "Of course we will. And if it doesn't work out with Wyn, we'll find some other options for you. Don't worry, Herne." She patted his shoulder. "We've got your back."

He smiled almost tremulously. "I thank you."

"Don't mention it," I said just as the bedroom door opened and Wyn stepped out, Lachlan looming behind him.

CHAPTER
FIFTEEN

Wyn glanced nervously at Herne before turning to me. "I, um, understand you have some questions for me?"

Right. I had a case, one that didn't involve scoring a date for an antlered guy who chased down and dismembered supernatural criminals for a living. I stood up and gestured to the sofa. "Would you like to sit?"

He checked with Lachlan, who nodded encouragingly, then moved over to perch on the edge of a sofa cushion. I retrieved my notepad from my bag and sat in the armchair.

I smiled at him—not too wide and not too smarmily. Professional. That was the ticket. "Some of these questions might be painful for you, so I apologize in advance. But it's important that we get at the truth, for your sake as well as... well, anyone else's. All right?"

He nodded. "I understand."

"Okay. Could you tell me when you initially encountered Reid Martinson?"

Wyn glanced at Lachlan nervously. "I don't remember the first time. He and his father were prominent in the supernatural community throughout the Pacific Northwest, though, so I imagine it was at some point after Lachlan and I moved here." He laced his fingers together in his lap. "I attended a number of social events on my own, since Lachlan wasn't... That is, he—"

"It's all right, Wyn," Lachlan said. "Matthew knows I'm not a bloke for parties. He'll not judge you."

I nodded. "I'm only trying to get an idea of the timeline. Do you remember when your…closer relationship with Reid began?"

His cheeks colored. "It was at a solstice celebration party. They'd invited both of us, but Lachlan had a booking he didn't want to cancel." Lachlan grunted, which I assumed was his way of agreeing. He'd told me about that party, but I wanted Wyn's take on it too. "For some reason, I couldn't get it out of my head, like I *had* to go. I couldn't make myself throw the invitation away."

"I expect it was bespelled," Eleri murmured as she sat on the other end of the sofa. "Both to entice you and to keep Lachlan away."

"That explains a lot," Wyn said bitterly. "The funny thing was that once I got to the party, I didn't enjoy myself at all. It was glittery and posh and full of people high up in supe society, but it felt so…so…" He made a helpless gesture with one hand. "Empty. False." He swallowed, his throat clicking. "Ominous."

"So you felt uncomfortable?" I asked.

"*So* uncomfortable," he said. "Then Reid came over and commented on it, that he would make it his job to see that I had a good time. He was charming, if a little too slick and hearty."

I clutched my pen tighter. This was it—the money question. "Did he offer you any food or drink?"

"I already had a glass of mineral water, but he made up a plate for me from the buffet."

"Do you remember what was on that plate?"

He wrinkled his brow, clearly trying to remember. "Olives, I think. Stuffed mushrooms. A bruschetta."

"On a baguette?" He nodded. "What else was on it?"

"A slice of tomato. A basil leaf."

"Cheese?"

He nodded. "Fresh mozzarella."

Bread and cheese. According to Cerys, once Wyn accepted it, he'd have had no choice but to accept Reid's advances. "And that's the night you first, um…"

He lifted one brow. "Cheated on my husband?"

Behind me, Herne made a choked sound, and I willed him to shut up. "Fell under the coercive spell."

Wyn nodded glumly. "For some reason, it felt perfectly reasonable to go with him, to leave Lachlan, to demand the sundering, to move into the Martinson's house."

"But you escaped. Do you remember how that happened?"

He bit his lip. "Reid hit me." Eleri and Herne both sucked in breaths at that, with an accompanying growl from Lachlan. "He'd done it before. But that night… It was the last straw."

More like the third blow. "And that's when you left?"

"It's like I couldn't get out of there fast enough. I shoved everything in my bags and ran." He glanced at Lachlan. "To Lachlan."

"Because you love him?" Okay, so that wasn't technically necessary for the investigation—I had what I needed to prove Wyn was a…a Dude *Annwn*: the bread and cheese, the third causeless blow, leaving with all his goods. This question was just for me. Well, for me and Lachlan.

Wyn smiled wanly at Lachlan. "Because I owed him an explanation. And because I trusted him to keep me safe as he'd promised to do at our handfasting. I knew he'd help me, and he did. So now it's my turn to help him." He met my gaze evenly. "What do you need me to do?

Could it be that easy? "I'd like you to come to the Quest offices with us."

Wyn's gaze turned sly, and he glanced between Lachlan and me. "Is that all?"

"That's the first step, the only one I can ask as a Quest investigator. As for other…issues, those are between you and Lachlan first." I glanced around the room. It didn't contain a lot of personal items. "Is this your, um, home?"

He shook his head. "No. It's…a safe house, you might say. A place of refuge, of reflection."

"Did you bring anything with you? Anything you need to pack?"

"A few things." He stood up. "It will only take me five minutes. If you'll excuse me?"

"Sure." I tucked my notepad away as Wyn disappeared into the bedroom, closing the door behind himself with a soft click but no additional locks. I glanced from Eleri to Lachlan. "So?" I asked softly. "I'm pretty sure he's Cerys's lost child."

Lachlan smirked at me. "He's no more a child than you are."

I glared at him. "I know that, and I'm glad you're admitting it." I gave him points for leaving off the *lad* that I could practically see waiting to pop out of his mouth. "But *child* doesn't denote age, only relationship."

Eleri was frowning at the door. "I don't know, though. Didn't you say that an oracle warned Cerys that her child was in danger and terrible things with a capital T were about to happen? Wyn seems like he's out of danger now. Abusive ex in the pokey. About to get unhitched from a stroppy selkie." Lachlan rolled his eyes at that. She grinned at him and jerked her head slightly at Herne, who was still slumped over his tea, apparently ignoring all of us. "Perhaps a new option on the table."

"Eleri." I laced my tone with warning. "Don't. Give the poor guy time to recover."

She shrugged. "Nothing helps recovery time like a rebound." She grinned wider. "Ask Sierra."

"You—"

The door opened and Wyn stepped out, once more in that trendy red coat that had caught Blair's eye and identified him as the original fish flinger. He had a small duffel slung over his shoulder. "I'm ready."

Lachlan strode over, his hand out. "I'll carry that for you."

Wyn gave Lachlan a fond but exasperated look. I could relate. "I'm not weak or fragile, Lachlan. I can carry it myself."

Lachlan scowled, but didn't push the matter. Apparently, I'd taught him something in the last couple of months: Grant your partner the courtesy of believing them capable.

I glanced from the mug in Herne's hand to my own discarded one on the coffee table to Eleri's next to the sink. "Do we need to wash up before we go?"

Wyn shook his head. "The housekeeping staff will take care of everything." He shrugged. "Brownies. You shouldn't insult them by insinuating they're not up to the job."

Interesting. So this place was the supe equivalent of an extended stay hotel? I had a sudden urge to check the fridge to see if it was actually a mini-bar. But Herne surged to his feet just then, so I didn't have the chance.

I craned my neck to peer past Wyn's shoulder into the bedroom. Nope, no door there either. I wondered briefly how *he'd* gotten inside without benefit of Herne's escort. Must be a *Corlun Dwr*-slash-Dude *Annwn* thing. I wish I felt comfortable enough with Wyn to ask him how the whole thing worked, but I wasn't quite there yet.

"If you would all please take hold of my cloak, I will transport us to Faerie."

"F-Faerie?" Wyn's voice wobbled. "I thought you said the Quest office."

"Faerie's just a waystation where we'll catch our, er, connecting flight," I said. "We won't be there for long."

"Do not fear." Herne's voice was gentler than I'd ever heard it. "None would dare harm you while you are under my protection."

I half expected Wyn to bolt back into the bedroom after Herne addressed him. However, he straightened his shoulders and took a firm handhold of cloak, although he didn't meet Herne's gaze.

The rest of us took our places and once again, we were... moving. This time, the trip wasn't quite so extended: No stars or planets, only one lake—or rather loch—and no fire whatsoever, probably because no searching was involved this time. Before I could count to ten, we were once more standing at the foot of the tor. I couldn't help but grin, because I'd never get over how *cool* all this stuff was.

When it wasn't totally terrifying, of course.

Wyn glanced nervously over his shoulder. "Could we go to your office now?"

"Of course." I turned to Herne. "Thank you. I really appreciate your help."

He inclined his head, although since all of us were well out of range of the antlers, he didn't skewer anybody. "I am ever in your debt. You may call upon me at any time. Jordan has my number." He faced Wyn and somehow morphed from an imposing meta-god to a middle schooler at his first dance, scuffing one booted foot in the moss. "I sincerely apologize for frightening you. It was not my intent."

Wyn, in what was the most daring thing I'd ever seen him do, patted Herne's arm. "It's all right. I understand."

Herne peeked up from under his eyebrows. "I really do think you're beautiful. You..." He swallowed and actually blushed. "You may call on me at any time as well. Perhaps we might share a meal."

Wyn's full lips parted in a quick inhale, startlement in his wide gray eyes. "I— I'd like that."

Then Herne was gone, in a swirl of silk and velvet.

Holy crap. I leaned over and whispered to Eleri. "I think Herne just asked Wyn on a date."

She smirked at me. "Told you."

"Yeah, but—" My cell phone rang inside my camera bag. "What the..." I'd never gotten a call inside Faerie before. I fumbled with the zipper and pulled it out to see Jordan's cell number on caller ID. "Hello?"

"Oh, Hugh. Thank goodness." His voice held relief and a touch of panic. "Will you be in today? Like soon?"

With Lachlan and Eleri gazing at me questioningly—although Wyn was still glancing over his shoulder as though he expected something to pounce on him at any moment—I mouthed *Jordan*. "We're almost there, but haven't you already left for the day? It was almost closing time before we left."

"That was *three days* ago," he wailed. "And there are *people* here. So many people."

My belly jolted. Three days? Herne had said we were *out of time*. Apparently, time hadn't waited for us to join it before moving on. "Isn't Zeke—"

"Zeke's not here. He's at some wedding out at Wildwood. Niall's still not back and Mal can't get here for some reason. I called Dr. MacLeod for…for backup, since he always knows what to do, but he hasn't arrived yet and I could really use the — Doop! No butt-sniffing! So hurry? Please?"

"We're on our way."

CHAPTER SIXTEEN

As soon as we stepped through the portal next to the vending machines, I heard it: loud voices and even louder barking. If Wyn was nervous in a virtually empty Faerie, I couldn't introduce him to his mother in the middle of whatever was going on in the lobby.

I turned to him with a forced smile. "Please don't be alarmed by the noise. I promise things are ordinarily much calmer here. We have a very comfortable conference room downstairs, and if you'd like to wait there, I'll sort out the situation in our lobby."

Wyn was looking a trifle white around the eyes, but he nodded.

"Lachlan? Would you please wait with him while Eleri and I assist Jordan?"

"Of course, la— Matthew. We'll be grand until you can join us."

We headed downstairs, Lachlan taking Wyn's elbow and peeling off on the third floor while Eleri and I barreled down the next flight to the lobby. As we hit the second floor landing, Bryce MacLeod was just coming up from the street entrance.

"What the hell is going on?" he said by way of greeting.

"Your guess is as good as mine. We've been gone. Apparently for three days, although I could swear it was an hour at most."

He rolled his eyes. "Fucking time differential is such a pain in the ass."

"Jordan said he called you, but why? Is Mal—"

"Mal," Bryce said through clenched teeth, "is at home, fuming because somehow Niall-freaking-O'Tierney has blocked him from entering his own freaking office when Cerys Glynn is here."

Eleri crept forward to peer into the lobby, but I couldn't do anything but goggle at Bryce. "That can happen? He can *do* that?"

"Apparently," he said dryly. "So much for collegial good will, eh?"

"But I thought the spells let anybody in who has legitimate business."

"And you'd think being the co-owner would give Mal legitimate business, but his freaking *business partner* doesn't trust him to keep his word."

I frowned, although Bryce's scowl had me beat by a factor of a hundred. "That doesn't seem like Niall."

"If you say so," he muttered.

Uh oh. From what Mal had let drop from time to time, Bryce had never really forgiven Gareth for treating Mal like crap for a couple of centuries, nor Niall for being the reason for said treatment. I'd thought things were getting better. Clearly I was wrong. Or else Niall was living up—or maybe down—to Bryce's worst expectations.

"Can Gareth talk to him?"

Bryce snorted. "Maybe. If Gareth could *find* him."

Now *that* was a shocker. I glanced at the lobby archway. The din inside hadn't diminished—and I had *never* heard Doop bark like that—but before we entered the fray, I needed to know whether my whole company was imploding. I gripped Bryce's elbow and towed him upstairs to the third-floor corridor. "What do you mean Gareth can't find him?"

Bryce sighed heavily and ran both hands through his hair, a habit that—along with his black-framed glasses—gave him a certain Egon Spengler vibe. "To be fair, Gareth hasn't had a chance to look. The band is playing at a wedding today."

"At Wildwood? The same one Zeke's at?"

He nodded. "Yes. Their manager is getting married. Niall was supposed to be there too, as Gareth's plus one, but he didn't show." He winced. "I probably don't need to tell you that pings one of Gareth's hot buttons, and his emotions always bleed through into his music, which in turn swamp his audience. I just hope the entire wedding party doesn't start wailing and rending their garments from sheer anguish."

I blinked. "Surely it won't be that bad."

"I hope not," he said, not sounding hopeful at all. "With luck, Gareth will remember he's a professional musician and keep it together for his manager's sake, but he's had centuries of selfish, prima donna behavior under his belt, so I have my doubts. If Niall's disappeared *again*—"

"I'm sure he'll be back. Maybe he's in Faerie. With Eamon. Trying to break the news about Cerys."

Bryce shook his head. "Nope. I checked with Eamon already. He hasn't seen Niall since the two of them met here to discuss Niall's freaking proposal to Gareth." Bryce practically growled. "Now, instead of proposing, he's ghosted. Again."

Downstairs, Doop began to howl. I winced. "I think we need to table the where's-Niall discussion until after we defuse whatever bomb is about to explode downstairs." I started down the steps. "Jordan called you?"

"He called Mal. But since Mal can't come..." He spread his hands, palms up. "You've got me instead."

Since Eleri was no longer stationed on the landing, I assumed she'd already joined the party inside. I inhaled and stepped through the archway.

And almost ran out again. Because holy crap. The place was in chaos. Jordan hadn't been kidding when he'd wailed about *so many people.*

He was crouched next to the desk, his arms circling Doop's neck, murmuring something into the hound's flattened red ears. Whatever it was didn't seem to be having much effect, but I couldn't blame the poor dog. He was barely more than a pup, after all, and this was *a lot*.

Cerys Glynn was indeed back, but instead of the demure, business-suited lady with magically dripping hair, she'd gone full on Cate Blanchett-black-eyed-Galadriel, her hair whipping around her face and the air rippling around her as she faced—of all people—Illiam Coutts.

Illiam was standing as stiff as a telephone pole, paying less attention to the angry *Gwraig Annwn* than he was to Eleri, who was glaring at him from next to Jordan.

Frang, my usual FTA driver, was cowering in the corner, his hands over his head and his gaze never leaving Doop. The only unfamiliar person was a slender, bespectacled brown-skinned man with curly dark hair and remarkable sea-green eyes who was standing next to Frang and regarding the room with a look of mingled alarm and amusement.

"Good lord," Bryce muttered.

"No kidding." I tried to make sense of the various shouted conversations. It wasn't easy.

Cerys (to Illiam): "Where is my child?"

Illiam (to Eleri): "You dishonor our heritage and flout my authority!"

Eleri (to Illiam): "Bite me."

Jordan (to Doop): "No barks."

Doop (to the world at large): "*Aaaaaawoooooo*"

I glanced at Bryce. "Do you suppose we can go for coffee and let things play out?"

He raised an eyebrow. "Unlikely."

"Excuse me?" I turned at the soft question, which undercut the volume of everything else. It was the unfamiliar man from the corner. "I'm Bartholomew Innes. Tholo, actually. Zeke Oz asked me to stop by?"

Oh. The changeling schoolteacher. I held out my hand. "Hugh Mann."

Tholo smiled crookedly. "That sounds like a nom de guerre to me."

I grimaced. "You're right. I'm actually Matt Steinitz, and things aren't usually so chaotic around here. You're not exactly seeing us at our best."

He chuckled. "No worries. I teach third grade at a school for supernatural children. This is almost peaceful by comparison." He glanced at the various combatants. "Is there anything I can do to help?"

"I'm not sure anybody could. Although if you could wait until things have settled down somewhat, there is somebody I'd like you to chat with. Someone with perhaps similar experiences to your own."

Tholo frowned thoughtfully as Cerys seemed to grow several inches and Illiam kept pace. "One of these people?" His glance lingered on Jordan, who had succeeded in redirecting Doop by offering him a Frisbee to guard.

"No. He's upstairs." I fervently hoped Lachlan had the sense to keep Wyn there. "So if you don't have anywhere to be for the next little while?"

He smiled at me. "It's Saturday. I'm completely free."

"Great." I glanced at the duergar in the room. "Did you come with Frang?"

Tholo shook his head. "No. He was here when I arrived. But he hasn't said much other than 'Don't let it get me.'"

"Yeah, Doop freaks him out a little." I tuned back in to the conversations.

Cerys (to Eleri): "You! You've been near my child!"

Illiam (to Jordan): "Keep that beast away from me!"

Jordan (to Illiam): "He's not a beast!"

Eleri (to Doop): "Sic him, boy."

Doop (to Illiam): *tinkle tinkle splat*

"Oh, brother," I muttered. I glanced at Bryce. "I don't suppose you've got a druid silence spell tucked in that vest of yours?"

Bryce patted the tactical vest I'd never seen him without, other than at his own wedding. "Unfortunately, no. Although it's clearly an application that's crying out for a solution."

"Guess it's up to me, then." I took a deep breath, stuck two fingers in my mouth, and whistled loud and long. The noise vanished other than a tiny whimper—which I wasn't sure came from Doop or Frang. "Could everybody please take a seat?"

Illiam drew himself up and pointed at Eleri. "She shouldn't be here."

I glared at him. "Yes, she should. She works here."

He grew an inch taller, and thorns sprouted from his ears. "That's—"

"They've been near my child," Galadriel-Cerys boomed. "So have you."

"We'll discuss that shortly, once we've sorted everybody else out. Jordan, I believe Doop has committed another indiscretion."

Jordan jumped to his feet. "Sorry, Hugh. I'll take care of it." He looked down at Doop. "Down. Stay."

Doop lowered himself to the floor next to the desk and laid his head on the Frisbee with a huff as Jordan pulled his cleaning supplies out of the Dooper bag—and, yeah, that name was gonna stick too.

I looked up at Frang. "You've never been inside the office before. Did you need something in particular?"

He lowered his hands, but he kept a wary eye on Doop. "Gareth told me to come here and collect Niall."

"He's not here," Jordan called as he mopped up hellhound pee. "Hasn't been here for three days."

I blinked. "He hasn't been back since we left? At all?"

Jordan shook his head, spritzing the carpet with his special green potion. "Nope. It's been pretty quiet." He glanced around the room. "Well, until now."

"Frang," I said, "there's no point in waiting here and being uncomfortable. Niall's not likely to show up here before he finds Gareth himself." At least I hoped not, if only for the sake of the Kendrick brothers' relationship. If both their significant others were ready to murder the other brother, the next family dinner would not be pleasant. "Why don't you head back to Faerie?"

"But Gareth told me—"

"If Niall shows up, I'll use an FTA voucher and contact you, okay? Promise."

With one last nervous glance at Doop, Frang nodded and left the lobby. His one-ton (more or less) footsteps made the building tremble as he climbed the stairs to the portal.

Okay, two down. I took a breath and faced Illiam again. "Mr. Coutts, I'm afraid any grievance you have regarding Eleri's employment will have to be referred to the King."

He snorted. "The *King*. He's no king of mine."

I frowned, glancing at Eleri. "Dryads are fae, right? I haven't got that wrong?"

She rolled her eyes. "We are. But *he* never even acknowledged the Celtic Unification, let alone the Seelie/Unseelie Convergence. I told you. OG."

Illiam looked down his nose at me. "I am loyal to my Queen and Consort, as any true Seelie fae should be."

"Uh, that would mean you're loyal to the King, since he's married to the Queen."

"That *pretender*," Illiam scoffed. "The true Consort is Rodric Luchullain."

Rodric Luchullain? Was this guy *serious*?

Eleri glared at him. "Luchullain was a homicidal maniac with delusions of grandeur and has been dead for almost a year. Get over yourself, Illiam."

He glared back. "Simply because you find our laws, our traditions, our very *roots* inconvenient to you doesn't mean you can dismiss them." His voice began to rise. "There are *reasons* for such laws. Our existence depends on them. They've stood us in good stead for millennia."

"Yeah," I said before Eleri had an aneurism, "but things change."

"They only change because people like *her*"—he jabbed a knobby finger at Eleri—"like *you*, like *him* flaunt them." I glanced over my shoulder to see who Illiam had been pointing to last and heaved an exasperated sigh. Cerys inhaled sharply, and I braced myself for hearing her break out another *You've been near my child!*

Because Lachlan was standing in the archway. Why had I ever imagined he'd be able to keep—as Mal and Niall always said—his big flipper out of things?

As Illiam stalked toward Lachlan, Wyn peered over his shoulder, his eyes wide. Great, just great. This hadn't been the way I wanted to introduce Wyn to Cerys, but I guess I had to deal with it now.

Illiam stopped, crowding Lachlan's personal space. "You refuse to answer your people's call."

"They don't need me," Lachlan growled, "but you need to stand down."

"If everyone would only embrace their nature, accept their responsibilities, our world, our kind, would not be teetering on the brink of disaster. Admit it! This profligate *change* that you all praise so highly is nothing more than an excuse for selfish, irresponsible behavior. For shirking. For needless rebellion." He crossed his arms. "I, on the other hand, have always, *always*, followed the old ways, adhered to the old laws. To the letter."

"From what I've heard," I said, "a lot of those old laws were total crap."

He rounded on me. "Hold your tongue, *human*. The only reason I countenance your presence here is because selkie-human pairings are—"

"Let me guess." I bared my teeth. "*Traditional.*"

He simply huffed and averted his gaze.

"You know the other thing about laws?" Anger was making it hard for me to speak. "They're contextual. They're made by people, whether supe or human, to address societal issues. That means they're just as likely to be flawed as the people who make them. And as for the people who enforce them? You can't count on them to interpret them the same way. So laws change all the time, because people change. Opinions change. The worlds change. Just because something's legal doesn't make it right."

"Humans." He sneered at me. "None of you have the fortitude to pick a path and stick to it."

"And thank goodness for that. Because some of those old paths led to really dark places. I like to think we're capable of learning. Of growing." I did my best to match his derisive expression. "You should understand the concept of growth, right? Since trees do that."

"That's..." His scowl deepened, which I hadn't thought was possible. He was starting to resemble one of those shriveled apple dolls that had always freaked me out when I was a kid. He looked down at his feet where Jordan was attempting to blot Doop's deposit off his shoes and pant leg.

Now, to be fair to the guy, which I wasn't exactly inclined to do, I don't think he *meant* to kick Jordan. I think he was probably just trying to avoid his ministrations. But the fact is, when Illiam jerked his leg away, Jordan lost his balance and toppled forward, and that knocked Illiam off-kilter. When he tried to catch himself, the toe of one loafer connected with Jordan's chest.

I hadn't known Doop could move that fast. I didn't even *see* him move. One moment he was lying next to the desk with his head pillowed on the Frisbee, and the next he was standing over a prone Jordan, eyes glowing gold, teeth bared, the fur on his spine standing straight up as he growled at Illiam.

Illiam paled, holding as still as, well, a petrified oak. From the way his mouth worked, he was probably trying to come up with some stupid threat, but if I were him, I'd have kept my mouth shut too.

Eleri, however, couldn't resist a jab. "You know, the *traditional* food of the *Cwn Annwn* is the flesh of traitors. If Doop is feeling peckish—"

"Eleri," I muttered, "not now. Jordan? You okay?"

"Yeah," he said. "Doop, stand down." Doop didn't seem inclined to move, his chest rumbling with a growl. "Doop!" Jordan's voice held that new note of authority he'd only discovered after he took charge of the hound. "Back off."

With what seemed like obvious reluctance, Doop moved aside, allowing Jordan to sit up, and though he dropped to his haunches, his fur didn't settle and his prodigious fangs were still on display.

"I shall report this," Illiam croaked. "There will be consequences. I shall demand satisfaction. Dangerous beasts at large—"

"He's not at large!" Jordan protested, scrambling to his feet. "And he's not dangerous. But he knows who the bad guys are, and he sure doesn't like *you*."

I patted the air with both hands. "Let's everyone take it easy. I promise we'll get things sorted. If you—"

"Husband," Wyn croaked as he flung himself against Lachlan's chest and clung there like a really handsome limpet. "Take me away from here. Take me home. Now."

CHAPTER SEVENTEEN

Lachlan met my gaze over Wyn's head, his eyes wide, his mouth stretched in a grimace. I expected him to peel Wyn off, but instead, he patted his back and said, "Of course, *mo ghràidh*."

I couldn't move, couldn't speak, couldn't do a damn thing as Doop growled at Illiam, Jordan soothed Doop, Illiam squawked at the universe, and Lachlan took Wyn's hand and led him up the stairs toward the portal.

"Hugh?" Eleri said softly. "Are you all right?"

No. I wasn't. Because if Wyn had changed his mind about severing the knot—and calling Lachlan *husband* and demanding to be taken *home* seemed a big fat clue that he had—then my fledgling relationship with Lachlan was over. Because Lachlan would never, ever break his handfasting vows unless Wyn agreed.

"Eleri. Do you know what *mo ghràidh* means?"

She winced and bit her lip. "I'm not entirely sure because it's Gaelic, not Welsh. But I think—sorry, Hugh—I think it means *my dear*."

My dear. Yet he called me *lad*.

Part of my life seemed to be crumbling before my eyes, and my heart had somehow forgotten how to beat properly. I sucked in an unsteady breath. I couldn't lose it. Not now. Not here. Because even if Lachlan walked away from me and back to

Wyn's arms, I still had this. I had my job. I had my place in the supernatural world, as occasionally uncertain as it was.

If I couldn't depend on anyone else, I could at least depend on myself.

So I turned around and faced the group in the lobby. Tholo was gazing thoughtfully after Lachlan and Wyn. He'd been so quiet that I'd forgotten he was there, particularly since everyone else was being so noisy. Jordan had retreated behind the desk with Doop, whose massive head was visible over the desktop, still glaring at Illiam. Without Doop in imminent danger of ripping out his throat, Illiam was regaining his stick-up-the-ass composure and glaring at Eleri as if this was all her fault.

I glanced at Cerys, ready to apologize to, you know, my *actual client*, especially since the man I was certain was her son had just skedaddled with my probably-ex-boyfriend without even a how-do-you-do. Considering that when I'd last paid attention to her, she'd been shrieking like a bean-sidhe about her child, I'd expected the same spooky-Galadriel vibe from her.

But instead, she was sitting in a chair in the corner, listing slightly to the side, one hand on her midsection over her *calon*, and the other pressed to her temple. She looked fragile and ill. For the first time since I'd met her, the droplets falling off her hair didn't vanish before pattering onto her suit.

"Cerys?" I approached her slowly and sank into the chair next to her. "I'm sorry things got so chaotic. I'd wanted to introduce you to the man who just left with Lachlan. His name is Wyn Ellis, and I believe he's your missing child."

"No," she murmured.

My middle turned to ice. If I wasn't right about this, if I didn't have my job, what did I have? "Are you sure? He identifies as a *Corlun Dwr*, but from what he's told us of a recent relationship, he bears all the earmarks of one of your nature."

She met my eyes then, and she seemed to shake off a little of her apparent shock. "I beg your pardon. I didn't intend to deny him. I believe he is my son. A *Gwr Annwn*." Aha! So that's the dude term. "But much as with Eamon, he doesn't need me. He's not the child I seek."

I gaped at her for a good ten seconds. "You mean there's *another one*?" Jeez, how many abusive relationships had she endured? My love life was sunshine and lollipops in comparison. "You gave birth a third time?"

She shook her head. "No. Only twice." She swallowed. "But I wasn't conscious for the second. I never saw the babe." She pressed her hand to her *calon*. "I can feel that there's another. One who *does* need me. The one whose trail the oracle urged me to find."

Holy crap. *Twins*? There were two guys out there who looked like Wyn? Not that twins were necessarily identical, or even the same gender. And if the other one was still in danger, that meant another abusive relationship.

I had no idea how to begin to look for this poor person, though. I suppose I could try Herne again, but he could only find people who were in some way traitors or oath-breakers. The only reason he'd been able to find Wyn had been because he'd cheated on Lachlan with Reid—even if he'd been coerced into it.

Expression hardening, Cerys rose out of her chair. She lifted one hand to point at Illiam again, and spooky Galadriel was back. "You! You knew! You've been near them both."

Illiam threw back his narrow shoulders and straightened his bow tie, but moisture dotted his hairline under his slicked back hair. Perspiration or sap? I'd have to ask Eleri later. "I refuse to remain in such a degenerate and ill-managed location."

"Nobody asked you to come in the first place," Eleri muttered.

He speared her with a glance. "I'll deal with you later. Now." He tugged his jacket hem, clearly trying to recover his stiff dignity, although with one pant leg still dark with Doop's piddle, he wasn't succeeding especially well. "I'll be going."

Oh, no you don't. I stood quickly. "Jordan, have Doop block the door."

"Sure thing, Hugh." Jordan flicked his fingers. "Doop. On guard."

Once again, I didn't see the hound move. He was simply *there*, standing braced on all four legs in the archway, eyes glowing and fur bristling. *Damn.* Jordan was one kick-ass puppy trainer.

"Mr. Coutts," I said, keeping my voice even with effort. "Please take a seat. I believe we have some questions for you." I glanced at Tholo. "I'm sorry to have wasted your time today. Perhaps we could chat again later. I'd like to hear your story."

Tholo smiled diffidently. "I don't wish to intrude, but I think I might be of assistance in this discussion. I was a missing child myself, if you recall. If you don't mind, I'd like to stay."

I shared a glance with Eleri and Jordan, who both shrugged, Jordan's cheeks a little pinker than usual. "Thank you, then. We'd be happy for your assistance."

"I object!" Illiam said. "I insist on leaving. Call off your cur at once."

Jordan narrowed his eyes. "You know, Doop couldn't stop you if you hadn't betrayed somebody or something. So go ahead. Give it a shot."

Eleri gazed at Jordan with obvious admiration. "Wow, Jordan. I'm really digging this new vindictive streak of yours."

He shrugged again and went even pinker. "It's not vindictive. Just the truth. Herne told me all about how the instinct to chase down traitors and oath-breakers is bred into Doop's DNA. We're working on coping mechanisms, but hey." He grinned. "It's *traditional*."

I chuckled, wheezing a little since my breathing hadn't evened out yet. "Touché. Now, Mr. Coutts, suppose you tell us what you know about Ms. Glynn's missing children."

For a moment, I thought he'd try to brazen it out. Call Jordan's bluff—although I suppose it was Doop's bluff really, and if I were feeling the least bit guilty, I wouldn't take a chance on those jaws.

Bryce, who'd been silent up until now, probably observing everything with his extra-special druid sight, said, "Give it up, Coutts. You're outgunned."

Coutts cast Bryce a resentful glare—apparently not *all* dryads viewed Bryce as the druid equivalent of a superstar—but nevertheless he sank into a chair, shoulders slumped in defeat. He crossed his legs, but made a face when his damp pants clung to his calf. I could have offered to get him a towel, but sue me. I wasn't feeling particularly generous at the moment.

"It had nothing to do with me," he grumbled. "I was simply in the wrong place at the wrong time."

"Explain," I said curtly. "Please."

"It was winter at my Outer World home, so I was in Faerie, merged with my tree." He drew himself up. "The oldest oak in Faerie."

Eleri snorted. "*All* the oaks in Faerie are old. You're not that special."

I could tell Illiam was winding up for an argument with her, so I said, "Eleri, if you don't mind?" She sighed, but nodded. I turned back to Illiam. "What happened?"

"A bauchan"—his nose wrinkled in distaste—"scurried out of the underbrush and laid two infants in the oak's exposed roots. How an Unseelie could encroach on my—"

"Let's not lose track of the main thread here," I said, unwilling to let Illiam's prejudices send us off on another tangent. "The bauchan simply abandoned two babies? Why didn't you help them?"

"I can hazard a guess," Tholo said, his voice hard. "He assumed they were changelings. Sickly fae children who would be switched with more robust human children from the Outer World." Tholo's thin face was grim. "That's *traditional*, isn't it, Mr. Coutts?"

Illiam fidgeted with his tie. "It wasn't my fault! I could tell they were weak, newly born. It wasn't my place to interfere."

"With helpless infants?" I growled. "You'd have let them die there, at your very feet?"

"I told you, it wasn't my place! Besides, the bauchan didn't disappear entirely. It hid in the bushes, waiting. And men showed up right after." He wrinkled his nose again. "One was Unseelie, so I was doubly glad I hadn't emerged. They took the babes away. That's all."

I drummed my fingers on my knee, considering Illiam's too-innocent expression. "If one was Unseelie, was the other Seelie?" Illiam pressed his lips together. "Come on, Mr. Coutts. If that was the case, you must have used it to rationalize your failure to act, since Seelie and Unseelie have only been one big dysfunctional Faerie family for the last year. Did that *untraditional* partnership push your bias buttons?"

He bristled. "No! And I am not biased! I'm *realistic*. I'm *traditional*."

"Ugh," Eleri said. "I'm getting really sick of that word."

"No kidding. Especially when it's used as an excuse for criminal negligence."

"I'm not a criminal! It wasn't my plot to hide the children from—" He clapped a hand over his mouth.

"Oho," I said. "So there *was* something else. What did you hear, Mr. Coutts? It's time to spill, because we have it on good authority"—I pointed at Doop—"that you're not blameless in this."

Doop, right on cue, growled low in this throat. *Good boy*.

Illiam gulped. "Th-the other man was... was human."

I blinked at that. A human in Faerie? It wasn't unheard of, but it was definitely unusual, especially if the human wasn't a prisoner of some kind, as Niall's mother had been. "Was the human a captive?"

"No. They appeared to be co-conspirators. Or at the least the human was a henchman of sorts. They were apparently working on the orders of the King."

I rubbed the bridge of my nose, a headache joining my pre-existing heartache condition. "This would be the old king. Tiarnach, right?"

Cerys whimpered and dropped back into her chair. "I should have known."

"What were the orders?" I asked.

"To...to hide the children until *she gives him what he wants,* I believe were the words."

"Tiarnach never could get over the loss of my dowry," Cerys moaned.

"The human was demanding payment, but the fae put him off," Illiam continued. "Which didn't please the human at all. *'What am I supposed to do with two puling brats? I never wanted them,'* I believe were his words."

I frowned. "Cerys. The father of your younger children. Was he fae?"

She shook her head. "No. He was human, but as my husband, was able to pass the portal if I willed it. He..." Her eyes glistened with unshed tears, although her hair dripped faster. "He relished life in Faerie, although he spent little time at my side there after I fell pregnant, preferring to carouse with the more disreputable sort at the Keep, gloating over the gold he won from them at games of chance."

"Do you think the human who took the children might have been your husband?"

Her eyes began to darken until they were pools of black. "That's why he struck me. So I would be forced to leave them behind as hostages to Tiarnach's greed." She rose from the chair, her hair whipping around her head. "He must have been in league with Tiarnach the whole time. He betrayed me, betrayed our children. For *gold.*"

CHAPTER EIGHTEEN

After Illiam confessed, I didn't see any reason to keep him around, especially since he kept sending poisonous glances toward Eleri, so I asked Bryce to escort him to the portal. I didn't specifically ask Bryce to kick the jerk's ass, but knowing Bryce, it went without saying.

With the part of my brain that wasn't occupied with the case and with whether Lachlan was out of my life for good, I wondered whether Illiam's actions were enough to get him ousted as Eleri's clan chief. The leaders of the supernatural community—most of them anyway—were a lot more progressive than they'd been before the Faerie Convergence and the Realm Accords. I had no notion how a dryad chief could be, well, *uprooted* from his position. I made a mental note to ask Bryce when Eleri wasn't around.

Since Jordan had to man the phones, once Bryce returned, a grim set to his mouth, the rest of us—Cerys, me, Bryce, Eleri, and Tholo, who showed no inclination to leave yet—settled down in the lobby chairs. I turned to Bryce. "Will Illiam's actions have any consequences?"

He took off his glasses, rubbed his eyes, and replaced them. "It depends."

"On what?"

"A lot of things. Including when the event occurred." He propped his elbows on his knees and looked at Cerys. "Your children were born in Faerie, correct?" She nodded. "Was Tiarnach still in power?"

She opened her mouth as if to reply, but then hesitated. "I… don't know. He may have already been deposed by Eamon by then." She shrugged. "I had a new husband, a human, and as a Seelie fae, Tiarnach was no longer relevant to my life. However, I think it was longer ago than that by the stars of Faerie."

I winced a little internally. I doubted Niall would be pleased at the inference that Eamon was also irrelevant to her. "I don't suppose we can judge by Wyn's apparent age either."

"No," Tholo said. "Not if the children were transported to the Outer World at different times. If the kidnappers kept the other child in Faerie, they might be quite a young child still. If they took the child into the Outer World directly, they could be well into middle age or even elderly."

"Like I said," Bryce grumbled, "the time differential is a pain in the ass."

Fabulous. Not only did we have a completely unknown person to track down, but we didn't know whether to look in a preschool or a retirement home. Or perhaps a cemetery. I rubbed at the ache in my chest. I didn't have a *calon*, but my heart was predicting catastrophe just the same. I glanced out the lobby window. From the slant of the light, it was barely past noon, even though I felt like I'd been up for the entire seventy-two hours we'd been out of pocket.

Bryce was right. Time differential was a pain in the ass.

Cerys was wringing her hands, water from her hair splotching the raw silk of her suit. "My son. Wyn. The one who was here. Has he any…difficulties?"

Other than being married to the guy I was pretty sure I was in love with? Oh wait. That was *my* difficulty, not his. "Not as far as I'm aware. Although…" I thought back on my first meeting with Lachlan, when he and Mal had gone after each other about Mal's one-night stand with Wyn. "I think he was searching for something in a partner that he wasn't completely successful in finding."

Eleri snorted. "You think? Anyone who'd fall for Reid Martinson—"

"That wasn't his fault," I said, maybe a little too sharply. "Reid took advantage of Wyn's *Gwr Annwn* nature. He—" My eyes widened, my jaw sagging. "Which means," I said slowly, "that he had to have known about it. But if *Wyn* didn't know, how could Reid have found out?"

"Pierce, probably," Eleri said. "He had some pretty unsavory connections. I mean, look at Ronnie Purl. Even without those, he could have scried it in a ritual flame. They were using Wyn to get to Lachlan, right?"

"Theoretically," I said. "But Reid wasn't the kind of guy who let go of anything once he got his mitts on it."

"Rather like Tiarnach, then," Cerys said.

"No wonder Wyn was holed up under the sea. Lake. Loch. Whatever." That brought up another question. How did Wyn get the magical key to that water-locked cottage in the first place? "Cerys, you said that for those who had the trick of it, your kind could move from one body of water to another. How do you learn the trick? Is it something passed on from one *Gwraig Annwn* to another? Is there some kind of supernatural airbnb listing that tells you where to go and how to get there? How do you breathe underwater, anyway?"

She smiled wanly. "We do not have gills such as fish do, if that is your meaning. We abide under the water in cottages not so different from those on land, although we must enter through the water." She commenced wringing her hands again. "If my children were not introduced to the water, to the way of it, when they were still young enough to recall swimming in the womb, they could have been irreparably harmed. In untold ways."

Wow, this kept getting better. The preschool or retirement home could be on land, under water, in Faerie, or in the Outer World. The only place it probably couldn't be was Sheol. From

Lachlan's experience there and in the forge, water-natured fae did *not* do well around fire, and I doubted the lava river was quite the same as good old Loch Ness.

And just like that, I hit the wall. That Wonderful Mug coffee seemed like years ago, back when I was full of hope and anticipation, imagining the day ending cozied up with Lachlan, planning our future. Technically, I suppose that day hadn't ever ended. Not for me. I'd hopscotched right over it while watching Nessie cavort in the water.

I ached for Lachlan, to see his face, to hear the burr in his voice when he said *Matthew* in the way nobody else did. But he was at *home*. With *his husband*. He hadn't hesitated for an instant when Wyn had asked, even calling him *mo ghràidh* again, while I was only *lad*.

"Get over yourself, Steinitz," I muttered. I needed to learn to manage on my own, without a selkie in reserve. I'd done it before I'd met Lachlan. I could do it again, heartache be damned.

Eleri looked at me quizzically. "Did you say something, Hugh?"

"Nope." I stood up. I'd follow up with Lachlan later. Find out whether Wyn's change of heart was permanent. If it was, Lachlan would never sever their knot. But if we'd actually broken up, I needed to hear those words explicitly from his stupid, gorgeous mouth.

That could wait, though. That *had* to wait, because I had a case to solve, and right now? I had approximately zero bandwidth to do it. "I'm sorry, Cerys, Tholo, Bryce, but I've got to call an end to this meeting."

"Are you giving up on finding my child?" The way Cerys's voice rang, I expected a little Galadriel smackdown.

"Not at all. But I need to regroup." And probably sleep for about twelve hours. "I've got some research to do before we can proceed. I'll be in touch as soon as I have a plan."

Bryce peered at me through narrowed eyes. I suspected he could see right through me, possibly literally. He'd given me a lot of information about druid sight, since he'd come into it so recently and still had that *Wow, isn't this cool?* factor that hit me about twenty times a day. "I'll see Tholo and Ms. Glynn out through the portal, shall I?" he asked.

Jordan jumped up. "Let me do that." Then he blushed. "I mean, I can do that. Since I'm an employee here and all. You don't have to bother, Dr. MacLeod."

Bryce smiled at Jordan fondly. Since he'd been one of Jordan's teachers for a couple of years, he'd had a lot of experience with the young were. "It's no trouble, Jordan." He cocked an eyebrow at the damp spot on the carpet. "And I suspect you have more, shall we say, remediation to do?"

Jordan ducked his head. "Oh. Right."

"Let me know if you need more cleaning solution, though." He chuckled. "Since Doop seems to be weaponizing his leg lifts, you might need it sooner than you think."

"It was a pleasure to meet you." Tholo shook my hand and Eleri's, although since Jordan was barricaded behind the reception desk with its dual monitors, he merely nodded to him and to Doop as well. "Please don't hesitate to contact me if you have any further questions or if my experiences can help in your investigation at all."

"I expect word soon of my child." Cerys took Bryce's offered arm, but she speared me with a glance that promised Galadriel in the future if I didn't come through.

"I'll contact you as soon as I know anything."

"See that you do. If I don't hear from you by tomorrow, I'll be back."

The three of them disappeared through the archway and up the stairs.

Eleri joined me as I stared moodily after them. "Has anything good *ever* followed that statement?"

"Probably not," I replied with a sigh. Although I'd have paid good money if Lachlan had said it before vanishing with Wyn.

She regarded me somberly. "What do you need from me, Hugh?" She grimaced. "I'd offer to surveil Lachlan and Wyn, but my camouflage won't be very effective if they've retreated to Lachlan's boat. Not many trees on the ocean."

"No. Give them both space. Since Cerys isn't interested in speaking with Wyn at the moment, he's not relevant to the case."

She gave me a disgusted look. "Who cares about the case? Lachlan just rode off into the sunset with the guy he was supposed to be divorcing, so—"

"Lachlan isn't a Quest employee," I said, my voice only wobbling a little. "He's also irrelevant to the case."

"But, Hugh." Jordan looked up from doctoring the carpet. "Your feelings are relevant." He glanced from me to Doop, who was gnawing on the Frisbee edge contentedly. "I've learned that working with Doop. Feelings can get in the way of sensible behavior. If we don't acknowledge them, they can lead to bad choices."

I shook my head. When Jordan was the one who had the keenest insight, it was time to take a break. "Thanks, Jordan. I appreciate the sentiment. But if the two of you don't mind, I really need to get some sleep."

"Sure, Hugh. No problem." He gestured to the desk with his rag. "I'll watch the phones. We'll be here if you need anything."

Eleri gripped my arm. "Anything. Anything at all, Hugh." She grinned. "And remember, I have the dryad attack squad at my disposal."

I chuckled tiredly. "Believe me. I know."

I grabbed my camera bag and trudged up the stairs. At the third floor landing, I hesitated. I should really go home and rest, like I'd told my colleagues I would. But as much as I loved my little rental house, I wasn't sure I was ready to face it. In anticipation of Lachlan being free, I'd hired a brownie cleaning service—another of the King's ideas about diversifying opportunities for his subjects—so the place would be sparkling clean, befitting a new start, a new life.

Nope. Couldn't do it. Not yet. Instead, I headed to my office. After my last couple of cases, I'd acquired a foldable cot so I could nap there if necessary. It was definitely necessary now, so I set my bag carefully on the desk and retrieved the cot from behind the door. I could only set it up if the door was closed and I pushed my guest chair behind the desk, but once it was deployed, I flopped into it, closed my eyes, and waited for sleep to take me down for the count.

CHAPTER NINETEEN

Sleep clearly wasn't with this particular program, because despite being so tired my eyelids felt like they were lined with sandpaper, I remained awake. After an hour or so of tossing and turning, my last sight of Lachlan's face popping up as soon as I closed said sandpaper eyelids, I sighed and sat up.

I scrabbled my cell phone off my desk and checked for messages. Nothing from Lachlan. Nothing from Mal or Niall either. I frowned. Mal I wasn't worried about, since he'd be with Bryce, who was a master—maybe literally—at relieving Mal's stress in ways I didn't really want to know about. But Niall...

Had he shown up at that wedding? He wasn't part of the band, but he spent *a lot* of time with them. As far as I knew, after he and Gareth got back together, the number of Hunter's Moon performances Niall had missed could be counted on one finger, if I wanted to round up. The band was playing at the wedding. The wedding of the band's manager. Surely Niall wouldn't blow it off completely.

I chewed on my lip. Zeke was in the wedding party, but he'd told me the ceremony was happening in the morning and it was past three now. He had little enough personal time, as conscientious as he was. But surely just a quick check-in call would be okay? I rationalized dialing his number. If he was busy or occupied with *his* boyfriend, he didn't have to answer, right?

Zeke answered on the second ring. "Hugh? Is everything okay?"

Trust Zeke to know something was up. One of his demon abilities was knowing a person's deepest desires, although he tried never to peek without permission. I didn't *think* that ability functioned unless he was face to face with his target. Although, maybe this call was unusual enough that he could deduce an issue without any demon insight at all.

"Yeah, sure, Zeke. Having a good time?"

"The best," he said happily.

"Great. Good. Just a quick question and I'll let you get back to the party."

"Of course."

I traced a pattern on the blanket bunched over my knees. "Is Niall there?"

Silence. Uh oh.

"Niall? I...haven't seen him," Zeke said carefully. I heard a rumble in the background, probably Hamish, Zeke's boyfriend, who never strayed far from his side if he could help it. "Hamish says he didn't show. Gareth is...worried."

I suspected that Gareth's worry might translate into an artistically temperamental meltdown. Thank goodness my boyfriend wasn't as highly strung.

Assuming Lachlan still *was* my boyfriend. I swallowed. "Okay. Thanks."

"Do you need me to come back?"

"No. Don't. You deserve a little fun. Sorry to bother you."

"It was no bother. I'll see you Monday?"

"You bet."

I disconnected the call. Niall MIA from Gareth was... unprecedented. Well, unprecedented if you didn't count his two centuries of incarceration in the forge before Gareth knew Niall's true identity. I debated contacting Niall myself, texting the number we used for Quest business. According to our office protocols, we never used that number unless the need was urgent. Niall ghosting Gareth? Seemed pretty urgent to me.

From what Mal had said, though, Niall's loyalty to his brother was almost as strong as his devotion to Gareth. What was it Jordan had said? *Feelings* could lead to bad choices. My vision swam, and I had to hold on to the edge of the cot. Niall wouldn't go so far as to prevent Cerys from locating her child out of allegiance to Eamon, would he?

However, if anyone could mount that kind of black op, it would be Niall. As an Unseelie prince and lifelong Keep rebel, he had connections among the less...savory fae elements. All Niall had to do was suppress information and he'd punish Cerys as he believed Eamon had been punished. But surely he couldn't resort to kidnapping a child. I hated to think the whole sins-of-the-parents was anywhere near Niall's wheelhouse.

I rubbed my gritty eyes. I had no idea if we were talking about a minor. But if the oracle was right and *somebody* was in danger, then relative age and past hurts—or even present ones, I admitted, thinking of Lachlan and Wyn—shouldn't matter. Averting that danger was the right thing to do.

And I wanted to believe—I *had* to believe—that Niall would do the right thing.

So I texted the number with a simple *Check in?*

My phone immediately vibrated with an incoming call, but my sigh of relief stalled and turned into a cough. Because it wasn't Niall. It was Zeke.

"Hugh, I *knew* something was wrong. I'll come back—"

"No! I mean it, Zeke. It's something only Niall can handle, related to my case. So really. Stay there. Enjoy the party. Let Hamish take you home and enjoy your day off tomorrow. Okay?"

"Okay." The way Zeke drew out the word made his doubt clear. But when somebody told him something—even when, like now, that something was a total lie—he believed them because he'd never lie himself. Honest people were by far the easiest to fool. "See you Monday."

After I ended the call, I contemplated texting Lachlan. If he and Wyn were on the boat, he wouldn't get it until he docked again. If they were at their old apartment, though... What would Wyn consider *home*?

Ugh. My head hurt, thoughts colliding like bumper cars. I needed something to take my mind off all this...this *stuff*. Something to reboot my brain and allow me to consider everything more rationally. Something calming. Something beautiful. Something wonderful.

Nessie.

I scrambled off the cot and pulled my camera out of the bag so I could pop the memory card and insert it into my computer. I uploaded the contents to our secure cloud storage, but kept a copy on my hard drive, too. When I launched the video, I couldn't help it—a smile spread over my face, and as Nessie wove and danced in the glow of her own scales, the knot in my belly started to unravel.

Now, I'm not totally unrealistic. I know there's ugliness and cruelty and injustice in the world—in all the worlds, for that matter, because supes can be just as selfish and narrow-minded as humans. I mean, look at Illiam, if you want an example. Or Reid Martinson, the abusive asshole who thought killing Lachlan was completely justified in his quest for power. Or Athaniel, who thought his accidental genetics made him superior to anybody else and gave him license to behave as he wished.

But in a world with Nessie? With Doop? With people like Zeke and Eleri and Jordan? There was enough wonder and beauty and delight to make me believe that the good would outweigh the bad in the end.

So I watched Nessie, one eye on the video progress bar, wishing it was twice as long. As it neared the end, I grabbed my mouse, ready to start it over and capture some stills—strictly for personal use, of course. But with thirty seconds left to go, the view swung from the window and panned shakily past Eleri and across the living room to land on Herne huddling over his tea.

I chuckled weakly. Poor Herne. If he'd had his eye on Wyn, his hopes might be dashed along with mine. Maybe if— *Hang on. What's that?*

I paused the playback and reversed it by ten seconds. *There.* Right in front of the mini-fridge. A distortion in the air, just like the one in Sheol that had marked the entrance to a dimensional pocket, the one where Herne and his pack had been trapped.

I leaned back in my chair, staring at the anomaly. I'd wondered how the cottage had gotten electricity at the bottom of a freaking loch. Come to think of it, the smoke from the fire had to vent somewhere, or everybody who stayed in the place would have succumbed to carbon monoxide poisoning. I'd always assumed, you know, *magic*, but in a general sense. Spells similar to the ones at Quest, which allowed only legitimate business through our doors.

Also, from all my observations and experience so far, I'd assumed that dimensional pockets and realms were discrete. In other words, that you, or some item, like Zeke's never-ending stash of office supplies, were either in one or not. A person or thing could pass through the portal—like Zeke retrieving a pencil or us using the door upstairs to enter Faerie. But you couldn't be in both at once, especially considering that damn time differential. Imagine if Zeke's hand got stuck in the office supply pocket and aged differently than the rest of his body. *Brrr.*

I knew there were exceptions. Faerie and the Outer World were pretty closely linked, and back in the day when Mal first met Bryce, there were environmental issues that leached from one to the other. The way I understood it, though, they had to be instantiated in each realm. But Faerie and the Outer World—not to mention Sheol—were vast. The smaller dimensional pockets weren't.

What if those pockets weren't discrete? What if you could daisy-chain them together, like a peer-to-peer network, or rooms in a shotgun-style apartment? Given its behavior, Wyn's hideaway was obviously a dimensional pocket, albeit a much more pleasant and stable one than the place I'd found Herne. Was Cerys's "trick" of moving from one underwater lair to another the result of such a dimensional chain?

Excitement fizzed in my veins, banishing my fatigue. This could be huge. In fact, it might be the answer to where the Disappeared had, well, disappeared to—slogging along the trans-dimensional equivalent of the Oregon Trail until they found a new place to settle.

On the other hand, maybe everyone in the supe community already knew about this stuff and I was just late to the party again.

I deflated a little, frowning at the monitor, at that ripple in the air. I suppose it was possible that the only thing on the other side of it was some kind of magical power substation, a place to plug in the fridge and vent the smoke. There was really no way to tell without plunging through, and who knew what might lurk on the other side?

This morning—this *relative* morning—when we were at Lake of the Freaking Beavers, Jordan had mentioned that Doop kept leaping into alternate dimensions and getting confused. He'd been able to detect Herne's pocket, but I'd kind of assumed that was because of Herne and the pack, not the existence of the dimension itself.

But what if I was wrong about all these assumptions? Maybe the answer to this case, to finding Cerys's child, was to start looking in places where they'd been sighted before and follow the trail. Sure, it wasn't exactly fresh, but there couldn't be that many places, right?

I jumped up from my chair and headed for the door, banging my shin on the edge of the cot. *Ow!* What time was it now? Had Jordan already left? I yanked open the door and raced down the hall. As I plunged down the stairs, I noted that it wasn't fully dark outside. Excellent. With luck, Jordan hadn't packed it in yet.

I heaved a relieved sigh when I stumbled into the lobby to find him just shouldering the Dooper bag. "Oh, hey, Hugh. Did you have a good nap?"

"Couldn't sleep." I glanced around, probably wildly, considering the trepidation that flickered over Jordan's face. "Is Eleri gone?"

"Yeah. She had a book club meeting."

Book club was Eleri's code for her subversive dryad cabal. Wonder what their cover book was this time: *The Secret Garden? The Magic Treehouse? Under Milk Wood?* Oh well. If this panned out, I could catch her up later. "Do you and Doop have plans this evening?"

"N-no." For an instant, he looked more worried, but then he brightened. "Do you have an assignment for us?"

"Maybe. Listen." I perched on the edge of the desk. "At the lake this morning—"

"You mean three days ago?"

"Yeah. That. You mentioned that Doop can traverse dimensional portals."

"Uh huh. I asked Herne about it later. He said it's something all *Cwn Annwn* can do, but mostly they're just following whatever prey they're pursuing along with him, so they don't get a lot of solo practice." He glanced down at Doop, who was sitting next to him, panting happily. "I worry that he's not getting the right kind of socialization for his abilities. Do you think I'm stunting him?" He scratched behind Doop's ears. "I don't want him to suffer."

I studied the hound's fluffy white coat, bright eyes, and the adoring look he gave Jordan. "Trust me, Jordan, he's not suffering at all. But I was wondering... Can you *ask* him to make the jump between dimensions rather than have it happen accidentally?"

"Oh, sure! In fact..." He reached into the back pocket of his jeans and pulled out his cell phone. "I asked Hector—you know Hector, right? One of the other guys at the Dog House?"

"He's the tech whiz, right?" Unfortunately, Hector's fascination and facility with manipulating the magic grid using modern tech got him in trouble now and then with supe leadership. But only when they found out about it.

"Yeah. I asked him to make a danger detector for me." He brandished his phone. The screen displayed a very simple graphic—just a green circle the size of a jar cap. "It's linked to the phone's camera. I just point it at the portal. If it stays green, it's safe: room on the other side, air to breathe, nobody around. If it's blue, there's people there, but they're not hostile. If it's red, don't go, because there's something on the other side that's dangerous." He wrinkled his nose. "It's not more specific than that, but Hector says he'll work on calibrating it to make it more sensitive."

I shook my head, chuckling. "We need to start calling Hector Q."

Jordan's brows drew together. "Why?"

I sighed. While a lot of ageless supes weren't up on recent cinematic references, I'd expected a youngster like Jordan to have encountered at least one James Bond film. *Time for that later.* "Never mind. I'd like to try something. It may lead nowhere, but it might help crack this case."

He seemed to grow two inches, his face glowing. "Whatever you need, Hugh." Then he turned serious. "As long as it doesn't put Doop in danger."

I pointed at his phone. "Green only. I promise."

I frowned, watching the light fade from the sky outside. The only problem was where to start. Maybe we should just test the theory first with a portal I already knew about. Sheol was out of the question, and Zeke's storage pocket was too small. The underwater cottage was our best bet, but to get back there, we'd need Herne.

I studied the window. It was almost dark, so traveling *on the night* could be on the table. Jordan had Herne's number, so why not? Since Wyn was with Lachlan, neither Herne nor I had any *other* plans for the evening.

"Take Doop out to do his business and then give your pal Herne a call," I said. "We're going on a road trip."

CHAPTER TWENTY

As I suspected, Herne was more than willing to take us back to the cottage under the loch. From the way he glanced around when we arrived, I imagined he had been hoping Wyn would be there. However, the place was empty, no fire in the grate, and no Nessie dancing outside the window. The refrigerator hummed, though, and when I checked in back of it, its cord was plugged into a wall outlet.

Not a lot of those in Faerie, let me tell you.

I took a couple of shots of the anomaly through my special lens and showed them to Herne and Jordan on the camera's display screen.

"See that? I figure there's something on the other side of that anomaly, something that's feeding power into this cottage. Could you check to see if it's safe for us to explore it?"

Jordan nodded enthusiastically. I held my breath while he dug out his phone and pointed at the anomaly. "Green! It's all good."

I looked at Herne. "Thank you for bringing us this far. You don't need to keep going with us if you'd rather not."

He shrugged. "There is naught else ahead of me."

I squinted at his antlers. "The thing is… Hector's app is configured for Jordan and Doop. A place that's an okay size for them might be a pinch for you."

Herne smiled. And was that an actual glint of mischief in his eyes? "As to that..." He lowered his head, gave it a brisk shake, and his rack clattered to the floor, causing Doop to leap back in alarm before creeping forward to sniff at it cautiously.

"Okay, then," Jordan said. "Everybody hang on." We each gripped the sturdy handle of the special harness Jordan had made for Doop when he'd first begun training him. "Doop, find it out!"

While traveling the night with Herne was smooth if visually disorienting, being yanked airborne by Doop was just as jarring as you'd expect. I stumbled a couple of steps before I caught my balance on the other side, my camera held tight to my chest as I avoided a collision with a tall metal shelf unit loaded with neat coils of cable, boxes of screws, cases of lightbulbs, and, for some reason, an inflatable life raft in its original box. A row of massive electrical panels lined the wall opposite the shelves. The place looked like the utility sub-basement for a downtown high-rise—I glanced at the raft box—in a flood plain.

"This is...interesting," Jordan said as he passed Doop a treat from his pocket. He sniffed the air, which was remarkably fresh and dust-free, and his smile bloomed. "Mr. Johnson's been here! I'd know his scent anywhere."

I suspected Jordan still harbored a crush on Rusty Johnson, since he frequently made dreamy comments about how much he looked like Thor when wielding a sledgehammer. Jordan had worked for Rusty's construction company in his first job outside his pack until an unfortunate incident with a nail gun. "I know Johnson Construction is handling the Sheol renovations, but I didn't realize they were working on supe infrastructure elsewhere too." I suppose it made sense. Faerie had to get its cell coverage somehow, Hector's magic-tapping apps notwithstanding.

I raised my camera and peered through the lens at the electrical panels. Sure enough, each one had at least one distortion, sometimes more, hovering in front of it, like a row of invisible access panels.

Holy crap! That's exactly what they were. Access panels. Access *portals*. Stabilized by this installation. I wondered briefly if it was itself a dimensional pocket or if it was a physical installation anchored under a skyscraper somewhere. I snorted. "Define physical, Hugh," I muttered. I needed to shed my human bias: Sheol was physical, or at least some of it was. Faerie was physical, even though it was a purely magical construct that resided in another dimension. It wasn't only the human world, *my* world, that was physical.

Over the top of my camera, I peered at one of the panels, the one closest to our entrance point. It had a label in multiple languages, similar to the signage we'd seen in Sheol on our visit there. Apparently, Rusty Johnson was meticulous in documenting his work sites. This one said *Loch Ness C*, and a frisson skated along my skin. Did that mean there was a Loch Ness A and B, possibly D through Z?

As exciting a prospect as that was, I had serious reservations. "Isn't this a little...insecure? I mean anybody who gets in here" —like us, for instance—"could barge into any of these places with no invitation and no warning." Again, like we were about to do.

"One can't traverse a portal willy-nilly," Herne said. "First, one must know it exists. Then one needs a reason. And a key."

"What kind of key?" Jordan asked.

"In my case, the nature of my prey is the only key I require. Their guilt, their intent, is my reason. Their presence on the other side of the portal proves its existence."

I gazed at Doop, who was sitting attentively at Jordan's feet. "You know," I said slowly, "I think we may be sitting in the presence of a master key."

Jordan glanced down at his hound. "You mean Doop?"

I nodded. "Because he can detect the portal already—existence—and the only reason he needs to jump through a portal is your command."

Jordan's eyes widened. "Wow," he breathed.

Of all the people in all the realms, I trusted Jordan's heart to do the right thing every time. His common sense? Maybe not so much. I gripped his shoulder. "Promise me you'll use your power for good, not evil."

He gulped. "I...I'll try. I promise."

"Aces." I paced along the row of panels, looking for something, anything, that might lead us to our next step. It seemed like the panels were split fairly evenly between what must be dimensional pockets in the Outer World—I didn't spot any for Sheol—and Faerie. There were also half a dozen that didn't appear to be connected to anything yet. Rusty must have constructed the control room for expansion. He'd only had about a year to work on this, after all.

"If you were a water sprite on the run," I muttered, "where would you hide?"

"In the water?" Jordan asked, still unusually subdued, probably from discovering he was in charge of a dog who, paradoxically, had the potential to be the greatest cat burglar in the multiverse.

"Perhaps not," Herne said. "It is true that...Wyn...retreated to an underwater refuge, but you are assuming two things."

I lifted an eyebrow. "Only two? That may be a record."

Herne gazed at me, clearly nonplussed. *Note to self: Rein in the snark with meta-gods.* "Sorry, Herne. Please continue."

"Recollect that the children were first taken in Faerie. They could have remained there or been transported elsewhere. We have no notion of their upbringing or their current circumstances. You assume that they are free to choose their hiding place. You also assume that they know they are a water sprite." His wide brow wrinkled. "Perhaps there's a third. That they are aware that they need to hide at all."

"Drat," I muttered. "Too many variables."

"Why not start at the beginning?" Jordan handed Doop another treat. "At Mr. Coutts's oak tree. I know it's been a while, but that's the only place we know for sure where both kids were. Maybe we can figure out who else has been there."

I blinked at him. "That's...actually a great idea. It might not pan out if the tree is in a high-traffic area, but we haven't got any other clue. Except..." I put the lens cap back on my camera in preparation for another Doop-rough ride. "How do we find the tree? I expect Eleri could tell us, but—"

"Oh! That's no problem!" Jordan pulled something out of another pocket and held it out. It was an oak leaf, a little brown around the edges. "Mr. Coutts sheds leaves when he's stressed."

I studied the leaf in Jordan's palm. "Why do you have it? You're not keeping trophies of Doop's indiscretions, are you?"

His face pinched with disgust. "No! I tossed the others with the clean-up rags, but this one was on the stairs." He shrugged. "I picked it up before we left. I didn't want to leave it for Zeke to deal with."

"Jordan," I said, "you never cease to amaze me."

He peered at me from under his floppy brown bangs. "Is that a good thing or a bad thing?"

"In this case, very, very good." I glanced at the electrical panels. "I doubt Mr. Traditional's tree is anywhere near one of these. Can Doop make a double hop?"

Herne took the leaf from Jordan. "Have no fear. I can take us to this tree on the night."

"Cool," I said, taking hold of Herne's cape. "Then beam us up, Scotty," I said.

Herne frowned at me, clearly puzzled. "I am of Windsor, not north of Hadrian's wall."

I sighed. No snark and no popular culture references. Got it. "Never mind. Let's go."

CHAPTER
TWENTY-ONE

And in a heartbeat, we were there, under the spreading branches of the biggest oak tree I'd ever seen, the violet Faerie sky almost invisible through its heavy canopy. I doubted Jordan and I together could span its gnarled trunk. Heck, some of its lowest branches were bigger around than my waist.

I squinted at a knothole at about my eye level. "He's not in there right now, is he? Illiam?"

Jordan shot me a mischievous grin. "One sure way to find out." Before I could stop him, he led Doop to the side of the tree and the dog lifted his leg. Nothing happened other than Herne shaking his head as Jordan gave Doop a pat. "Nope. Nobody home."

I narrowed my eyes. "You told me once that you could tell if a dryad was inside a tree by the scent. Was that leg lift necessary?"

He flushed. "Not really." His eyebrows bunched. "But that guy made me mad. And in Faerie, trees *like* to get watered by the Cwn Annwn. Herne told me."

Herne nodded solemnly. "It is true. Their essence keeps certain pests away."

"Fine. Let's see if we can find out anything else before Doop dilutes all the evidence."

While Herne circled the tree and Doop sniffed its roots, I backed out from under it, far enough away to get some long shots of the area. I worked my way around, making sure I caught it from all angles, which wasn't that easy considering the heavy underbrush in the area. I really hoped Faerie didn't have a poison ivy equivalent.

The oak was big enough that there weren't a lot of other trees very close to it. However, I frowned when I noted at least two air distortions. Unlike the magical utility basement, the tree wouldn't need electrical or power connections. And neither Zeke nor either of my bosses had ever mentioned that Faerie had its own pocket dimensions. So were these...mini wormholes? Internal conduits to other spots in Faerie or the Outer World? That's the only thing I could think of.

So where did these lead?

Herne joined me as I pondered the problem. "I can discern traces of the babes, and of a human. But the only fae whose essence I detect is the dryad who claims this tree.

"Illiam," I said. "It's his tree, so that's no surprise, as is the lack of traffic." I snorted. "He probably pops out of the tree and shouts *"Get off my lawn!"* if anybody gets within ten feet."

Jordan joined us, Doop trotting at his side. "Doop can track somebody he knows, so he could find Illiam. But who would want to?"

"Nobody, if they had a choice." I showed him the photo with the anomalies. "Could you point Hector's app at these and see whether it's okay to follow them?"

"Sure thing, Hugh!" He pulled out his phone and aimed it at the first anomaly. "Green!" He moved on to the second and frowned. "I've never seen *purple* before. I have no idea what that means. I wonder if Hector upgraded the app? Want me to call him?"

"Maybe later. Let's give this one a shot first, since it's got a green light."

We clustered around Doop, gripping his harness, and Jordan called, "Doop! Find it out!"

Another teeth-rattling jerk and airborne leap and we landed, stumbling on a rough stone floor. I caught myself with one hand on a wall covered with a huge tapestry that had seen better days —probably about five hundred years ago.

"Ooof!" Jordan grunted. "What's this chair stuffed with, anyway?"

I glanced over at him. He'd tumbled onto an armchair upholstered in threadbare purple velvet. Even under Jordan's sprawling figure, I could tell that its seat sagged halfway to the floor. More of its filling dropped onto the stones with a *whump* as Jordan pushed himself up.

I turned slowly in place, scanning the room. Four walls, made of massive, rough-hewn stone bricks, were hung with tapestries that stretched from floor to very high ceiling. Only one window —a narrow clerestory high up on one wall, far higher than even Frang's eye level—let in enough dim light to see. Barely. The chair Jordan had landed in was one of several other equally decrepit furnishings clustered in the middle of the room as though they'd been shoved there to get them out of the way.

Among those furnishings was a worm-eaten cradle.

The only door was in the wall opposite me, so I skirted the edge of the room, taking shots as I paced toward it.

"I know this place," Herne said. "We are in the Keep."

I stopped. "The Keep? As in *the Keep*? The home of the King and Queen?"

Herne nodded. "Formerly the seat of the Unseelie King whom I pursued to his doom."

Cheery conversationalist, our Herne. I peered upward. The heavy ceiling beams were festooned with cobwebs. From what Niall had said of the lesser fae who staffed the Keep, they were meticulous in their work, although now they took pride in it for the satisfaction of a job well done. In Tiarnach's day, they'd done it out of self-preservation. Tiarnach had certain standards where his own comfort and convenience were concerned, and wasn't shy about expressing his disapproval. With his sword.

So why would they neglect this room? True, it was chilly and windowless and uninviting. The wide hearth was full of ash and clearly hadn't held a fire for some time. The nasty furniture I've already mentioned. But it could be put to better use than, well, *nothing*. Although I suppose if your home was a magical castle, you probably had enough available living space that you could afford to ignore the less desirable spots. "Location, location, location," I murmured.

"Hugh?" I jerked my head up at Jordan's wavery voice. "Could you come here for a minute please?"

He and Doop were in the opposite corner, in front of a small alcove that I hadn't noticed before, Jordan's hand on Doop's harness to hold him in place. I hurried over to him, dodging a sagging brocade chaise. When he pointed a shaking finger, I crouched down and peered inside.

A ragged blanket. A tumble of small wooden blocks. A tarnished cup lying on its side. That wasn't what sent a chill down my spine, though. Along both sides of the opening, metal rings were driven into the stone. I reached out a tentative finger, but didn't touch. I knew what had to have been mounted in those brackets.

"They locked them in," I murmured, anger flaring in my middle. "It wasn't enough to stick them in this cold, cheerless room. They had to lock them in a freaking baby jail."

Because it was absolutely clear to me that at least one child had been here. Cerys's child? Perhaps. But why not both? Why not two cradles, two cups, two blankets? Had one of them been taken elsewhere in the beginning, or had this been a prison for other children at other times?

"Master?"

I whirled at the soft query from the doorway. I knew enough about fae species by now to recognize a bauchan by their moss-green hair and pebbly brown skin. Not only that, but I recognized *this* bauchan. "Heilyn?"

Heilyn tugged their forelock. "Yes, Master."

I grimaced. "I'm not your master, Heilyn. You don't need to call me that."

"A term of respect, Master Hugh, no more." Heilyn regarded us gravely, their gaze traveling from Jordan and Doop to Herne. "We have waited so long for this. For you."

"We?" I asked.

"Those of us who were here in those dark days." Their eyes, the gold of old bronze, met mine, and I noticed with a jolt that two other sets of eyes were regarding me, one over Heilyn's shoulder and one atop their head. "We have waited, and we have hoped, and here you are. Come to seek justice at last."

"Justice for who?" I asked.

Another mini-Heilyn scrambled around Heilyn's middle to cling to their jerkin. "For the little ones. The lost ones." They rested a protective hand over the kid on their chest. "For the children."

I clamped down *hard* on my fury. Yes, it looked like a lead had played out, but this...this atrocity... Well, it was a lot, you know? Maybe too much.

"How many children have passed through this room?" I asked.

For some reason, the bauchans didn't move past the doorway. "So many. But more in the old days, when fae moved more freely in the Outer World, and took what they wanted with no one to say them nay."

"You mean changelings?"

They nodded. "Yes. But the last was different. Not taken to nurture, to raise, but as"—they made a sharp gesture with one hand—"leverage."

That made sense. Cerys said that Tiarnach wanted her dowry back, and what better way than by holding her newborns hostage? That tactic hadn't worked well with Eamon, but he'd been older by then, had presumably already been introduced to the water in the way that had so concerned Cerys about her twins. Besides, from everything I'd heard, Tiarnach, blinded as he was by his own narcissism, wasn't one to learn from past mistakes.

"Did Tiarnach order the kidnapping?" Heilyn nodded again. "Did anybody else know about it?"

"The guards. The nursemaid." Heilyn shuddered. "She begged them not to take the little one from her, but they ignored her cries." They bowed their head. "They killed her then. As *unnecessary*."

I winced. "Is that why this room is so unkempt?"

"Aye. None have tidied the place since the day they took her to the block."

"Because you're honoring her memory?"

They pointed to the ground. "Because we cannot enter."

I moved closer and noticed the line of rock salt and herbs that spanned the doorway. I frowned down at it. "That looks fresh."

"Wards aren't swept away by time, Master Hugh."

I swung my camera to my back. "Maybe not. But they can be swept away by me."

I crouched and brushed the crap aside with both hands into two piles, one at each side of the doorway. As soon as the threshold was clear, Heilyn rushed in. Their kids immediately leaped off their parent and made a beeline for Doop who, with a long-suffering expression, let them swarm onto his back.

I rested my arms on my thighs as I watched them squeak in glee, burrowing in Doop's fur. Belatedly, I realized I hadn't photographed this part of the room yet. Jeez, some investigator I was. Heilyn's footprints, small, webbed, and four-toed, were visible on the dusty floor, but they weren't the only ones. Before it could be disturbed further, I stood.

"If you all wouldn't mind staying right where you are for a moment?"

When all of them agreed—even Herne smiling indulgently at the little bauchans' antics—I hurriedly photographed the scene. Walls, furniture, floor.

When I was shooting Jordan's purple chair, I noticed something on the floor nearly obscured by a clump of horsehair that had fallen out with the force of his unceremonious arrival.

The bit I could see from under the ratty stuffing was bright white, an anomaly in a room where everything else was dim, dingy, and dusty. I stowed my camera away and extracted a pair of the nitrile gloves I kept in my bag. Gingerly, I shifted the fallen material aside, trying not to disturb what lay underneath.

And what lay underneath, you ask? Two oak leaves—not exactly a shocker by now, right? But alongside them was something I'd never, ever expected to find in Faerie: a white plastic bag. Not just any white plastic bag, mind you. A white plastic bag sporting the Stuff 'n' Things logo. And inside?

An all-too-familiar faded rainbow beanie folded over Niall O'Tierney's Quest business card.

CHAPTER
TWENTY-TWO

For a moment, all I could do was stare at the beanie, my mind whirling, facts coalescing in my numb brain. Lachlan, his shifting ability compromised in fresh water. Jordan, complaining about underwater sight being distorted. Floyd, whose resentment and neglect never translated into physical violence.

Blair.

But Eleri had said Blair wasn't a supe, that she couldn't detect a calon. Could she have been wrong?

I knew there were precedents for calon anomalies. Rusty Johnson's impaired calon prevented him from shifting. Changeling schoolteacher Tholo Innes had fae blood but no identifiable fae nature. Hell, Niall himself was able to mask his fae nature when he tried. I doubted Blair was hiding intentionally, but could their calon be compromised, a result of their mixed human/fae parentage?

Cerys's children, assuming they took after her, were fresh water beings, and she'd feared that without proper exposure to water, they might suffer some unspecified difficulty. Might they be adversely affected by salt or salt water? If one of them hadn't gotten the right, er, post-natal dip, could it affect their vision or other senses? Their calon's functionality?

That could account for Blair's salt sensitivity, their prosopagnosia, Eleri's inability to identify them as a supe. Although…

When Blair visited our offices the first time a few weeks ago, I'd assumed the Quest protective spells had admitted them as Lachlan's sidecar, a nonthreatening guest. But what if the spells had recognized Blair for their own sake, because they weren't entirely human and had every right to be there?

Furthermore, if Blair wasn't Cerys's child, why would somebody target them specifically, as the presence of their beanie suggested? I was as certain Blair was the missing kid as I'd been about Wyn—and while that hadn't played out the way I'd anticipated, you've got to admit I was right. Maybe Floyd was Cerys's ex and their father, or maybe he was just the human who'd been pressed into service by Tiarnach. Heck, he might not even be aware that Tiarnach was dead.

The presence of Niall's business card tangled my thoughts even more. Was it a coincidence? Zeke kept all our business cards in handy holders on his desk, so anyone who'd been in the office could have taken one at any time. Had somebody—presumably Illiam, given the telltale oak leaves—simply discarded it as unnecessary? Or had that somebody contacted Niall to give them the identity of the person who could rock the O'Tierney family yet again?

Could I believe something so heinous about my boss? That Niall would target Blair in a misguided attempt to punish Cerys on behalf of his brother, who may not even care anymore about that long-ago abandonment? I had severe doubts about whether Niall had bothered to ask Eamon how he felt before he activated his battle protective mode, since Lachlan had a similar tendency.

Supes. God. They were the *worst* at communicating their feelings.

However, it might not be too late. I didn't know for sure that Niall had done something unforgivable. Blair could be perfectly safe at home—or as safe as possible with their loser of a father figure. And who knows? Maybe I was wrong about Blair's parentage, and when Cerys met them, she'd pull another *not that one* on me. Regardless, I didn't want to waste any more time.

"Herne," I croaked.

He looked up, and whatever he saw in my face banished his smile. He reached me in two huge strides. "What's amiss?"

"Your tracking ability. If someone fits within your definition of traitor or oath breaker, you can find them, right?"

He nodded. "When the Wild Hunt rides, I can pursue any at will. At other times, however, the quarry must first be identified by name."

"So if I give you a name..." I had to swallow twice, because my throat seemed full of my heart. "If I give you a name, could you tell me whether they qualify? Whether they'd be on your radar? And why?"

Again he nodded, his brows bunched together. "Aye."

Here goes nothing. "Niall O'Tierney."

Herne's eyes went wide and his gloved hands fisted at his sides. "Are you certain?" When I nodded, he stared at me for another moment before lifting his chin, nostrils flaring, as if seeking a scent in the dusty air. I held my breath for one second, two, three. He met my gaze and shook his head.

I clenched my eyes shut for an instant. *Meta-god, remember. Be specific.* "Okay, does that mean *Sorry, Hugh, he's a despicable kidnapper,* or *No, he's clear?*"

"The second. The only stain on the prince's soul is his deception of the bard. And since the bard has forgiven him, the stain no longer calls to me."

I'm not too proud to admit that relief literally knocked me on my ass in a puff of dust. "Thank goodness. Oh, thank goodness." I'd learned by now that not all things in the supe world were sweetness and light, but despite Niall's recent theatrics, I trusted him. Believed bone-deep that he was a good man—well, good fae—who was dedicated to the welfare of the community and to doing the right thing.

But my relief wasn't the important thing. I scrambled to my feet and held out the oak leaf. "Can you tell if this is Illiam's?"

Herne took it carefully between thumb and forefinger. "Aye." A fire kindled in his eyes. "And he *is* my rightful prey."

I flexed my hands, my fingers tingling. I wasn't a combative sort—not physically anyway—but I'd have given a lot right then to land three blows on Illiam's supercilious nose. Unfortunately, I didn't think we'd be lucky enough to for him to disappear, along with all his worldly goods and antiquated attitudes. "We'll be paying him a little visit, then. But first, Jordan?"

Jordan looked up as one of Heilyn's youngsters scampered up his shoulder and leaped off onto Doop as if diving onto a cushy mattress or into a pile of autumn leaves. "Yes, Hugh?"

"You called me when I was in Faerie before. Does that mean my phone works here now?"

He flinched. "Um. Not really. Mostly."

"Does yours?"

His gaze skittered away from me. "Maybe?"

I took a breath to corral my impatience. "I'm not going to bust Hector, although I think he needs to come clean with Bryce if not the entire supe council. Could you please call Lachlan?"

"I— I can try."

As Jordan pulled out his phone, I took a moment to hope that Lachlan wasn't so involved with Wyn that he'd fail to answer. For the second time, I held my breath. *One one thousand. Two one thousand.*

"Hey, Lachlan. It's me. Jordan." He shot me a thumbs-up. "I think Hugh wants to talk to you." When he paused, I could hear Lachlan's basso rumble from across the room. "Oh, because we're in Faerie and his phone doesn't work here." Another rumble, which made Jordan's eyes widen before he held out the phone to me.

"Asked you why your phone worked here, did he?" I murmured and took it as Jordan flushed. "Lachlan." I had to clear my throat, which had gone thick again. "I don't want to invade your privacy—"

"Bollocks to that, Matthew. It's no invasion. You can call on me at any time." He chuckled, although it sounded a little tight. "I expected to hear from you long since, if I'm to be honest."

Honesty? Yeah, I could do with some of that, but my personal life could wait. "Where are you right now?"

"On the boat—"

"Damn," I muttered.

"At the dock."

My shoulders sagged with relief. "Okay. Good. That's great. You need to get to Blair. Right away. Right now."

"Blair? Why—"

"No time for questions now. Just get to Blair and keep them safe. Bring them to the boat if you can. We'll meet you there."

"Matthew—"

"We'll talk later. Just *get Blair*."

When I returned Jordan's phone, everyone in the room, from Herne to Heilyn's kids, was staring at me with wide eyes.

"Wow," Jordan breathed. "I never knew you could be so *forceful*, Hugh."

"Yeah, well, I've got a reason. I'm pretty sure I know who Cerys's missing kid is." I pointed to the oak leaf in Herne's hand. "I'll wager anything you like that Illiam wasn't just an innocent bystander in the original kidnapping. He was in it up to his knothole. That's why you couldn't detect another fae under the oak. Because Illiam was the only fae involved."

"But why?" Jordan plucked the little bauchans off Doop and handed them—much to their dismay—back to their parent. "Eleri says he's an isolationist. If he's such a stickler for tradition, why would he get involved in something like that?"

"We can ask him that when we confront him, but I suspect isolationism is precisely the reason. The children were half human, most likely conceived at the order of the old Unseelie King. In his hurry to get them out from under his tree, Illiam probably didn't realize he was turning himself into one of the conspirators."

No wonder he'd suddenly showed up on our doorstep after Cerys engaged our services. He was afraid he'd be exposed and forced to face the consequences.

I grabbed a handful of Herne's cloak. "Heilyn, do you think you could leave this room as it is for a little while longer? We need to preserve as much of the evidence as we can."

"Aye, Master Hugh." At a soft word, probably Welsh, the kids took their places on Heilyn's back. "I will guard the door myself."

"Thank you, my friend. Jordan? We're leaving."

Jordan took a firm grip on Doop's harness with one hand and Herne's cloak with the other, and a heartbeat later, we were standing in a lace-curtained Victorian sitting room, its furniture festooned with antimacassars, and its many fussy shelf units holding enough china bric-à-brac to start a Hummel museum.

Illiam was dusting one of said china figures, his back to the room, but when he heard Doop's growl, he spun around and the figure dropped to the floor with a crash. "I didn't do it!" he cried.

"Didn't do what, exactly?" I asked, my jaw tight. "Because if you're about to claim you didn't enable the kidnapping of two innocent children, you might as well save your breath."

He drew himself up, but despite the way he looked down his long nose at me, his hands were shaking. "Those weren't *innocent children*. They were *changelings*."

"Really? Incoming or outgoing?"

His eyebrows bunched in confusion. "What do you mean?"

"I mean, who were they being exchanged for?"

"That's irrelevant. Such things are outside a dryad's purview. We succor plants, not people."

I ground my teeth together. "Sorry, but that's not gonna fly. Two infants were left on your roots. What happened to them?"

"How should I know?

"Because you were *there!*" I roared, prompting a side-eye from Doop, although he didn't stop growling at Illiam. In fact, he added a tiny lunge and snap of his jaws, although he was still well out of reach of any sensitive part of Illiam's anatomy, more's the pity.

Illiam squealed and cringed. "The human! The human claimed he was acting under the orders of the Unseelie King. But when I insisted he leave, he only took one brat. He blathered on about the King and the Keep, so I assume that's where he went."

"Oh, come off it." My phone vibrated in my jacket pocket, but I ignored it. "You know perfectly well where he went." I pulled out an oak leaf and waggled it in front of his nose. "You went there too."

He paled. "I didn't! Not then! I couldn't. The roots of my tree extended into the Unseelie sphere, but I would never follow the human into Unseelie lands. What would people say?"

"If you saved a baby, they'd probably say you were a good guy," Jordan said.

"Be silent, werewolf!" Illiam snapped. Bad move on his part because Doop did *not* take kindly to anyone dissing Jordan. His growl grew in volume.

"So let me get this straight," I said. "You washed your hands of two babies, who, by the way, were not technically changelings since they weren't supposed to be exchanged for anything other than Cerys's dowry—so you wouldn't be *embarrassed?*"

"You don't understand."

My phone vibrated again. "Oh, trust me. I understand narcissistic sociopaths all too well." I'd run into more of them than I'd cared to over our last few cases. "What happened to the other child? The one the guy left under your tree?"

With Doop's growl getting louder, Illiam edged farther away, backing up against one of his fussy shelf units and sending his china ornaments wobbling. "I...I passed it to another fae. A Seelie, as was only proper."

"Let me guess," I said. "One residing in the Outer World? Near Loch Ness?"

"I didn't want it near me!" he cried. "Besides, it obviously didn't belong in Faerie or it wouldn't have been discarded."

"For Pete's sake." I didn't bother to hide my disgust. "You act like a baby is less important than one of these ugly china figures. At least you take care of them."

He bridled. "They're not ugly."

"Eye of the beholder," I muttered. "Okay, who did you pass the baby to? What kind of fae?"

"A glaistig." Indignation flickered across his face. "She had the audacity to insist on an annual tribute of gold, delivered in person, in return. As though the creature were my responsibility!"

"Imagine that," I said dryly as I racked my brain for the reference. Glaistig, glaistig. *Ah.* Scottish water spirit with a decidedly good cop/bad cop reputation. I hoped the kid— probably Wyn, since Blair seemed saddled with a human caretaker—had gotten one of the benevolent ones. "So why poke your nose into it again after all this time?" He didn't say anything, just crossed his arms and stared at his feet. "No comment? Then I'll take a guess. You found out that Cerys Glynn was a Quest client and you were afraid we'd uncover your less than honorable actions."

"Quest," he spat. "Don't flatter yourself."

I frowned. If not Quest, then— I snapped my fingers. "Eleri. You found out she'd met Blair, didn't you?" He must have gotten the scoop from those gossipy zoo schefflera plants Eleri had complained about. "That's why you were trying to force her to quit. Because we were getting too close. And you didn't want to be *embarrassed*."

Jordan's phone rang. He winced as he fumbled it out of his pocket. "Sorry, Hugh. I'll decline—" His eyes met mine. "It's Lachlan."

Crap. He was probably the one who'd been calling me. "Go ahead and answer."

He nodded, keeping his gaze locked with mine. "Hey, Lachlan. Yeah, he's here." He handed me the phone.

"Lachlan?"

Lachlan didn't waste time on polite greetings. "Blair's missing. So's their sorry excuse for a father."

"Hold on." I glared at Illiam. "Did you tip him off? Your human accomplice?"

"He's not my *accomplice*. He's nothing but an Unseelie tool."

"There are no Unseelie any more, you spineless twit! Where is he? And where's Blair?"

"I'm sure I don't know," Illiam said with an attempt at his signature disdain.

"Try again." I brandished the Stuff 'n' Things bag. "I kinda doubt you shop there, because judging by this room, there's nothing you need and a lot that you don't. Your crony was with you at the Keep, in that room where Blair was captive until something happened to spook you both and send you to the Outer World." He pressed his lips together and turned to the window again, clearly trying to pretend we weren't there. I huffed an exasperated breath and raised Jordan's phone again. "He's not talking," I told Lachlan.

"I'll bloody well *make* him talk." Lachlan didn't bother to keep his fury buried. "Any wanker low enough to victimize a child—"

"Two children," I said. "I think he hoped Wyn would drown after he gave him to a glaistig."

Lachlan's snort held obvious smug satisfaction. "His bad luck that being dunked underwater was exactly what Wyn needed. Can't drown a *Plant Annwn*."

"*Plant Annwn*?"

"That's what they call the bairns, since they're not husbands or wives. But I don't trust Blair's father. He's kept Blair so terrified of the authorities that Blair won't think to try to get away. He's got the poor mite completely brainwashed."

"I don't know about that." I smiled despite my worry. "Blair found you, didn't they? Somehow they knew you were a safe haven."

Lachlan groaned. "We've got to find them, Matthew. Tell me where you are and I'll—"

A telltale *tinkle tinkle splot* interrupted Lachlan's tirade. Sure enough, when I turned, Doop was just lowering his leg, and Illiam's face was a mask of outrage and disgust. "Hold tight, Lachlan. I'll text you as soon as we've got a location." I handed the phone back to Jordan. "Did you encourage him?"

Jordan blinked at me, the picture of innocence. "Would I do that?"

"Yes." I grinned at him. "Good work." I turned back to Illiam, who was reaching for an umbrella in a stand shaped like an oak stump. Unless it really was an oak stump. "If you're thinking about hitting the hound, Mr. Coutts, you'd better think twice. He's much faster than you are."

"Get out of my house. All of you. You have no right—"

"Guess again." I pointed at Herne, who'd stayed as silent as one of Coutts's knock-off Tiffany floor lamps. "You might not recognize him without the antlers, but may I introduce you to Herne the Hunter?" Herne inclined his head and Illiam blanched. "You're on his radar, pal. And this is your last chance for a plea bargain. I don't think I need to tell you that Herne's hounds will do a lot more than pee on your shoes if they catch you."

I could tell he was thinking about making a break for it, but seriously, how stupid was that? He spent half his time as a *tree*, for Pete's sake. No way he could outrun Doop, let alone Herne and his pack.

His shoulders finally slumped. "Fine." He looked down at his wet loafers. "But could I please change my clothes first?"

CHAPTER
TWENTY-THREE

Once Illiam gave us coordinates of the place he'd arranged for Blair's alleged father to hide out—a seedy motel between Tillamook and Garibaldi—I asked Jordan to convey the information to Lachlan while I called Cerys. I told Jordan to ask Lachlan to bring Wyn along. I even called Bryce and asked him to pass our location to the King. I wasn't sure the King would be interested, but I wanted to give him the chance to make his own decisions rather than having Niall keep him in the dark. I texted Niall too, not that I expected him to answer now when he hadn't bothered before.

Might as well make this one big dysfunctional family party.

Herne materialized us in an extremely cramped gas station bathroom across Highway 101 from the motel.

"Doop!" Jordan said. "No butt-sniffing."

"I don't think he did it on purpose," I said, angling myself so Doop's snout wasn't in my crotch. "There's not much room to maneuver in here. Herne, could you please get the door?"

We spilled out onto the buckled asphalt, earning a startled glance from the station attendant who was filling up the tank of a battered pickup. An instant later, the bathroom door opened again, and Lachlan emerged with Wyn. The attendant dropped the fuel nozzle. When Cerys stepped out next, he turned and ran inside, leaving the customer frowning after him until he took a gander at our motley crew under the harsh station lights. Then he hightailed it after the attendant.

While Wyn cowered behind Lachlan, Cerys looked around eagerly, and Doop sniffed at a clump of weeds growing through a crack in the asphalt, I kept my eye on the bathroom door. But neither the King nor Niall emerged, so I sighed and pointed across the street. "Thataway."

We trooped across the road, Herne keeping a firm grip on Illiam's elbow, in case he tried to bolt. I didn't think it was necessary. The guy looked completely cowed by now, resigned to his fate, or else hoping to avoid a worse one.

I scanned the two-story building, its stucco showing the wear of an ill-maintained seaside structure, the paint on its turquoise doors cracked and peeling.

I glanced at Herne. "Which room?"

With no hesitation, he pointed to the balcony, the room second from the end. "There. Two twelve."

"Shall we?" We all clanged up the metal staircase. I was surprised it didn't collapse under our combined weight. Lachlan kept glancing at me, and then looking away. I sighed and kept Herne and Cerys between us. Whatever conversation we were about to have—and we *would* have one—I didn't want it to interfere with getting Blair out safely.

We reached the door: one meta-god, two water sprites, one selkie, one dryad, one werewolf, one hellhound, and me. We'd scared the bejeebus out of the gas station attendant and his customer. What kind of reaction would we spark in a scared kid and a desperate human asshole whose agenda was still a mystery?

I beckoned everyone to retreat toward the stairway a bit and leaned in, my voice low. "I think Lachlan should be the one to knock on the door. He's the only one here who won't frighten Blair, and at least Floyd knows him."

"Why should I bother to knock?" Lachlan growled.

I glared at him. "If you break down the door, not only will you scare Blair, but you might prompt Floyd to do something stupid." I glanced around at the motel. "Stupid*er*. Our main goal here is Blair's safety. Everything else is gravy." I checked on Cerys, whose hair was starting to whip around her shoulders although she hadn't gone full Galadriel yet. "Keep in mind that Blair's been raised as a human. They have no idea about Faerie or the supe community. So if you don't want to send them into catatonia, keep a lid on the woo-woo stuff, okay?"

She stared at me haughtily for a moment, but then nodded and her hair stopped doing its water ballet.

"Okay, Lachlan. Go."

When he strode down the cracked concrete, Wyn made an abortive attempt to hold on to him, then edged behind Herne, on the other side from Illiam.

Lachlan knocked on the door. "Blair?" His voice was low and gentle. "It's me, jo. Lachlan. Could you open the door please?"

I braced myself, because if he was given the least excuse, I didn't trust Lachlan not to break door and alleged father both. But when the door cracked open, its flimsy security chain *chink*ing, it was Blair who peeked out.

"Lachlan?" they whispered. "What are you doing here? How did you find me?" Their eyes behind those new glasses widened. "Are they after us? Child services?"

"No, jo." Lachlan crouched down so he was eye level with Blair, who then got a good look at the rest of our posse. "Not child services. But some other people who'd love to meet you." He glanced over his shoulder at Illiam. "Well, not him. But everyone else. Where's your da?"

"Asleep," Blair said, their eyes glued to Doop. "He stopped at that liquor store down the road."

Lachlan glanced at me. "Blair, you trust me, don't you? Me and Matthew?"

Blair nodded hesitantly. "But that other man is here. The one who threw the fish."

Wyn colored at that, hiding his face against Herne's impressive biceps. *Interesting.*

"Yes. But he only threw the one, and he's sorry for it. I'm going to ask you to trust me now, jo. Trust that I'm telling you the truth and that you'll be safe, no matter what. Can you do that?"

Blair glanced over their shoulder, probably at their father in his drunken stupor. "Do you promise?"

"I do. And so does Matthew."

"Absolutely," I said. "We're here for you, Blair. All your friends."

"And your family," said a deep voice behind me, and I turned to see the King himself, Eamon O'Tierney, dressed in, of all things, a kelly green UO hoodie and jeans, his hand on Wyn's shoulder and smiling at Blair with tears welling in his eyes.

CHAPTER
TWENTY-FOUR

Things got a little crazy after that. Blair was suitably impressed by Eamon, although they were still a little wary of both him and Cerys. Luckily, Doop went all derpy puppy, charming Blair enough that they agreed to walk down to the parking lot with Jordan and Eamon. The rest of us crowded into the mildewy motel room and gathered around Floyd's bed, where he lay with his mouth agape, snoring like a bandsaw.

I glanced at Cerys, who was regarding him with distaste. "Were you actually married to this guy?"

She huffed. "What can I tell you? Bread and cheese. The gods have a lot to answer for."

Lachlan whacked Floyd on the foot. "Wake up, you wanker. It's over."

Floyd blinked bleary, blood-shot eyes, peering around in confusion for a moment. But then he spotted Illiam and Cerys and jerked upright. I'd expected him to cringe or bluster, but instead a look of such joy spread over his dissolute face that you'd think we'd just told him he'd won the lottery. "I can go back? The King is satisfied?"

I glanced at the others, all of whom seemed equally in the dark. "Satisfied with what?"

"The money." He pointed at Cerys. "The money she stole. The King promised that as soon as she returned it, I could come back."

"Back where?" I asked, mystified.

He glared at me as though I were an idiot. "To the palace, of course. To Fairyland."

Crap. I grimaced. Cerys had said her ex had reveled in Unseelie court life. I'd also heard stories about humans who'd consumed Faerie food pining for it afterward forever. Technically, this guy was Tiarnach's victim, too. I really didn't want to feel sorry for him, not after the way he'd treated Blair, not to mention Cerys.

He glanced around, brow furrowed. "I did as he asked. I took care of that brat, and never hit it, even though it earned it."

Okay, no worries about undue sympathy from me. Cerys, considering Galadriel was coming out to play again, had even less. "I am taking my child."

He sneered at her. "Good riddance to you and it both." He peered around at the rest of us, his gaze landing on Herne as the person with the most obvious power. "Will you take me back now? He"—he jerked his nose at Illiam—"wouldn't let me stay."

"I'll take you," Herne said. "I'll take you both, although I doubt you'll be pleased with the destination." He turned to Wyn, smiling almost shyly. "And afterward, perhaps we can have that meal."

Wyn nodded, equally shyly. "I'd like that."

I blinked, my gaze skipping between Herne, Wyn, and Lachlan. "What—"

"Later," Lachlan murmured. "We'll talk later, Matthew, and I'll tell you all about it."

I had to be satisfied with that for the moment.

Not only then, however, but the next two days as well, because while the supe community managed to keep itself hidden in plain sight in the human world, retrieving a supe from said world and bringing them to the other side was a little trickier, especially with a child who was already on the social services radar.

It was accomplished, however, although nobody would tell me exactly how. Cerys had officially been granted custody of Blair as her biological child, even though Blair wasn't ready to go with her quite yet. Instead, she, Wyn, and Blair—along with Lachlan—were in Faerie, guests of His Majesty at the Keep, although I sincerely hoped all of them had cheerier quarters than Blair's last royal bedroom.

Or so Zeke told me, anyway. So far, Lachlan hadn't shown up again, although he'd sent me sporadic texts, promising that he'd see me soon. I had to be content with that, since I didn't really have much choice.

I was filling out my final report on Cerys's case when there was a knock on my open door. I looked up to see Niall, looking unsurprisingly sheepish. I leaned back in my chair, lifting an eyebrow. "So. Decided to crawl out from under your rock, have you?"

He groaned, scrubbing both hands over his face. "You have no idea how accurate that is."

"Come on, Niall. Where the heck have you been? And has Gareth let you back in the bedroom after your little disappearing act?"

He dropped into my visitor's chair, and although his eyes were bloodshot, he looked...at peace. "I may have gone on a bender with some old duergar buddies. Their drink of choice is deadly. They dumped me in the Keep dungeons to sleep it off, and Heilyn didn't find me until this morning." He winced. "Sorry about the tantrum."

"Everything okay now?"

He spread his hands, palms up. "Maybe? Eamon's annoyed with me for making decisions on his behalf, but he's so chuffed to have two more half-siblings that he's not taking the piss out of me too much. He and Cerys are...doing all right, mostly because they're both trying to be whatever Blair needs." He shook his head. "It's a lot to take in, finding out you've got a mother you never knew, that you're not quite human, that you've got a twin nearly a generation older, and that your other brother's a king. No wonder the poor wee kiddo's clinging to Lachlan like he's their last hope of dinner. Alun's working with them, though, and he says things are going well."

"And Gareth?"

He smirked. "None of your business." He stood up. "But seriously, mate, thank you. You did a brilliant job on this case with absolutely no support from me or Mal. If I haven't said it enough, we're lucky to have you here." He saluted with two fingers. "Cheers."

When he turned, the door was blocked by a very familiar broad shouldered, long-haired figure. "Ah, Brodie. About time you showed up. Done lurking around my brother's Keep and getting underfoot?"

"For now," Lachlan said. "Blair's doing better. Bonding with Heilyn and those bairns of theirs. That Tholo bloke from the supe school is helping out too. Gives me a chance to check in here." He gestured for Niall to step out of my office. "With Matthew. In private."

Niall winked at me. "Never let it be said that I can't take a hint." He disappeared down the hall as Lachlan closed the door behind him.

"Lachlan," I said, my mouth dry. "I wasn't sure when I'd see you." Or *if* I'd see him, despite his cryptic texts.

He grimaced, chagrin twisting his mouth. "I'm sorry about that. But until Blair felt comfortable, I couldn't leave them. I'm the only link they've got to what they've always known."

"I understand."

His mouth turned up in a sly smile. "I've got something for you."

I studied him. He was wearing his usual sea-green anorak with a cream-colored fisherman's sweater underneath and a pair of what could only be described as dad jeans. His hands were empty.

"What? The promise never to wear those jeans again?"

"Nay. This." He reached into his anorak pocket and pulled out a fistful of...something. He held his hand over my desk and let it fall. I stared at the tangled mess of ribbons, green and blue. "What's this?"

"It's done, Matthew." He jerked his chin at the ribbons. "The sundering ceremony. My knot is severed."

The fluttering in my belly could have lifted me into the air. "You're free?" I croaked. "But Wyn called you husband. Said he wanted you to take him home."

"Aye. But that's because he spotted Illiam." He sat down in my visitor's chair and extended one big palm. I took it. "All this time, we thought he was hiding from Reid and Pierce. But that wasn't it at all. He's been hiding from Illiam all his life, since every time Illiam visited, he'd get shunted to another place, another foster fae, some of them kinder than others. Before he married me, when he tried it on with Mal Kendrick? He was looking for someone to protect him. To keep him safe from Illiam, although he never really understood what Illiam wanted with him. He thought he'd found safety with me, but Reid managed to capture him anyway because he had no idea of his true nature."

I thought about the coy looks Wyn had been casting Herne, and the heated ones Herne had tossed right back. "I'm guessing he's found a better protector now."

Lachlan chuckled. "It could be, although it's early days yet."

I nodded, a lump in my throat. I'd been waiting for this almost since the day we'd met. But now that our relationship was in our grasp, I had a sudden urge to dive under my desk. I hadn't dated anyone seriously since my mid-twenties when my boyfriend of two years had dumped me because—and I quote—I was getting too weird. He wasn't entirely wrong—I'd started pursuing cryptid photography by then, and after he'd left, I'd thrown myself into it fully, both from sincere interest and as a coping mechanism.

But now, over ten years later, did I even know how to begin?

There was nothing standing between us anymore. But when Lachlan held out his arms, his eyes full of obvious intent, I hesitated.

"Matthew?" His tone held confusion, as well it might. We'd been waiting for this moment for what felt like forever.

"What if it's no good?" I whispered. "What if we're not compatible? What if you think I'm a terrible kisser? What if I think *you're* a terrible kisser? What if—"

"Matthew." He stood, and I scrambled out of my chair too, and when he paced toward me, I only backed up a step. Okay, two. Because this was *it*. "Nobody knows everything about another right away. But I've seen your heart, as big as the sea, and it fits beside mine like the two were forged in the same fire. Two parts of one whole, waiting until we could join them together again."

"That's really poetic, Lachlan," I said crossly, "but I'm talking *logistics*. Practicality. *Reality*."

"So am I." He reached out slowly and took my hands. "Whatever we don't know about each other now, we'll learn. If I do something you don't like, you'll tell me, and I'll do the same. We don't have to be perfect *now*. We only need to be willing to work toward that goal, every day, from now on."

"Easy for you to say," I grumbled.

"No. Not easy at all." He cradled my face in his big hands. "But for you, I'm willing to put in the work."

Then he kissed me.

Lachlan's kiss was *so* not terrible. His lips as soft and plush as they looked, his taste a little salty, a little sweet. Judging from the way he hummed against my mouth, he didn't think *my* kiss was terrible either.

Thank goodness for that, because you know what?

Although that first kiss was absolutely perfect and one hundred percent worth waiting since September for, I refused to wait another nanosecond before claiming another.

So I didn't. And neither did he.

WHAT'S NEXT?

❖

CHECK OUT MATT'S NEXT CASE!

DEATH ON DENIAL

DOA becomes BRB when this client goes MIA...

When I agreed to accompany my selkie boyfriend on a private boat trip, I didn't realize the invitation included a swim. In the Pacific. In November. Naked. And I certainly didn't expect to have our swim derailed the instant I got in the water— holy crap, that's *c-c-cold*—by a literal boatload of selkie clan leaders.

Climbing out of the water in front of them—did I mention naked? Yeah, way to make a brilliant first impression. Then things get worse: I get served. Not in the metaphorical sense, either. Nope, I'm being sued.

By Death.

Well, not Death precisely, but an Ankou—a Celtic psychopomp who escorts the departed to their final destinations. This guy is miffed that his workload has increased exponentially, which he blames on my actions in Sheol on an earlier case. I'm not about to take the heat when eons of shady demon shenanigans finally come home to roost, but here at Quest Investigations, we aid any and all supernatural folk in need—especially if they'll drop their specious lawsuits against the agency's lone human.

When the Ankou skips out on us, though, all hell breaks loose. Because without anyone to lead them on, the dearly departed become *nearly* departed and stick around to party hearty. Now it's not just the selkie leaders complicating my love life—it's the ex-living as well.

And when one of the ex-living decides not to remain ex? Things get really complicated, not to mention deadly.

Dammit.

DEATH
ON
DENIAL

"You want me to do *what*?" I goggled at my boyfriend, whose resting grump face was softened by a hopeful half-smile.

"Go on a wee swim with me." Lachlan held up a bundle of glossy short brown fur the same color as the darker streaks in his hair. "In my skin." He ducked his chin, pink infusing his tanned cheeks. "You've never seen me in my skin."

And *that*, my friends, was the problem. I *wanted* to see him in his skin, every six-foot-six, broad-shouldered, beefcake-gorgeous inch of it. But he wasn't talking about *that* skin. Nope, he was talking about his *seal* skin. As in, sometimes he's a seal—and not the Navy kind. Nope, an actual seal.

Yeah, my boyfriend. The selkie. Not only a selkie, but the selkie *king*, if he'd ever bother to take the throne.

And me? Just a human ex-tabloid photographer who somehow got lucky enough to earn a place with the supernatural community, land a job with Quest Investigations, and score a super- hot boyfriend who sometimes had flippers instead of hands and feet. #lifegoals.

"I've already seen you in your seal skin," I grumbled as I braced myself against the rocking of *Cridhe na Mara*, Lachlan's cabin cruiser, "so that argument won't fly."

His eyebrow, the one bisected with the thin white scar, shot up. "You have? When?"

"During our first case." It was my turn to blush. "I, um, watched you when you went over the side after we found that dead herring in your berth."

Lachlan grinned, altogether too smug. "See anything you like?"

"Don't be a jerk. You know I did." My eyes widened. "You, um, replaced that mattress, right?"

His grin faded, and he laid his seal skin across the pilot's chair so he could rest his hands on my shoulders. "Of course I did. Your comfort is everything to me, Matthew." He nudged my chin up and kissed me softly. "If I have my way, you'll never be anything but safe, happy, and contented."

I peered up at him, smiling slyly. "I'd be *very* comfortable, happy, and contented if you took me to bed right now." What can I say? I've got zero game.

"I want you to understand me. To know me. This"—he gestured to the ocean and to his seal skin—"is who I am. It's a part of me."

"You know what's a part of me?" I said testily. "The part that objects to voluntary hypothermia."

"Matthew." My shiver wasn't entirely the result of the throaty burr in Lachlan's voice when he said my name, because the wind off the water was freaking *cold*, even in the shelter of the pilot house. "I need you to embrace *all* of me."

I hugged my jacket tighter to my chest. "I'd rather embrace all of you in front of a nice cozy fire. Or better yet, in a nice cozy bed."

Lachlan chuckled and stroked my face. "We'll get there. I promise. And the sooner you're in the sea, the sooner I'll be able to keep you warm."

I leaned into his touch and sighed. *Just remember that berth waiting for us down below.* "Fine. Let's get this over with."

His smile nearly melted my bones, and if I got a little distracted watching him take off his clothes, baring every inch—and there were a *lot* of inches, if you get my drift—of his skin? Trust me, if you could have seen him, you'd have been drooling too. If I wasn't so obsessed with all things supernatural, I'd have almost objected when he pulled on his seal skin. Except he bent over to slip it over his feet, so you know, there was *that*. I might have whimpered.

He heard me, because of course he did, and paused with the skin pulled up to his waist. "Matthew?

"Right. Sorry." I glanced around the pilot house. "Where's my wetsuit? Is it below?"

His brows drew together in confusion. "There's no wetsuit."

"A drysuit then?" That would be better. I'd heard that wetsuits weren't exactly toasty.

"Matthew." He approached me again, his lower half encased in that fur that looked softer than silk and fit him like, well, a second skin. He still had the usual number of legs and feet—he couldn't shift unless he was actually in the ocean—and his chest was bare and dusted with *another* kind of fur. *Rawr.* "I thought you understood. All your skin must be touched by the sea, as is mine."

My jaw sagged. "Are you *serious* right now? You want me to go in the water *naked*?" My ears heated, a sure sign my anger was about to get the better of me. "It's *November*, Lachlan." I pointed over the stern, where the Oregon coast was still visible across what now seemed a vast expanse of choppy waves. "And that's the freaking *Pacific Ocean*."

"Aye." His tone implied that this was all completely reasonable. Which, in case you haven't gotten the memo, it was not.

I scrubbed my hands over my face, my fingers catching in my beard, which could probably use a trim. "Lachlan. This day has already been hell. Literally."

He frowned. "What do you mean?"

"I mean that before I showed up at the marina to meet you, I spent the morning in Sheol—"

"You went to Sheol?" His frown morphed into full-on glower. "Why?"

"I was at a photoshoot with Paimon."

"That demon who wanted you to update his headshots?"

"If only headshots were all he wanted," I muttered.

Lachlan actually growled. "Did that wanker put his hands on you?"

"Down, boy. No. But he decided he wanted some swimsuit shots. Next to the lava river, because, and I quote, *It makes my eyes pop.*" I shuddered. My eyes were the ones doing the popping, because Paimon had, er, more than the usual number of appendages barely contained in his tiny speedo. He claimed the extra equipment saved on refraction time. Which, you know, good for Paimon, assuming his partners were on board and had given full, non-coerced consent, but whatever.

My problem was I still hadn't encountered *Lachlan's* appendage. We'd had a number of *extremely* hot make-out sessions, but every time we started to take it further, we got interrupted. If it wasn't a call from my office—and Quest had been inundated with a rash of minor theft cases lately—it was one of Lachlan's regular fishing tour bookings, or another of his visits to support our friend Blair as they got settled in Faerie.

Now, I don't begrudge Lachlan's time with Blair. I mean, Blair was doing great, considering they'd just relocated to a home in another freaking *dimension*, but it was definitely a lot, and Lachlan was their only link to the life they'd always known. And I certainly couldn't fault him for attending to his job, since my workload in the last few weeks had been the cockblocking culprit just as often.

But I'd been certain when he invited me on this private outing on his boat that we'd finally have the chance for some mutual naked exploration in the berth—with its brand new mattress, thank you, Lachlan.

I'd never dreamed that our first skin-to-skin encounter would be under the freaking Pacific. The instant I put a toe in that water, my junk would retreat so far inside my body I'd need to go spelunking to find it.

Not the best first impression to lay on a new lover.

I tried another tactic. "But there could be sharks. Great whites. You said so yourself."

Lachlan chuckled. "Aye, sharks live in these waters, but they won't come near us." He cradled my face in his hands. "Selkies may look like seals, but inside, we're still supes. We've our own protections, our own magic, to keep the beasties at bay. You'll be safe with me. Always."

Drat. There went that argument. "What if someone sees me?" We were beyond the jetty, anchored in the open ocean, but with land still in sight... I really didn't want to be flashing my fish-belly white butt to somebody with a high-powered telescope— or worse, a drone camera. Hell, a few years ago, if I'd had a hint that something like Lachlan's shift was about to happen, I'd have been the one with the long-distance recording equipment.

"No one will see you, *mo cridhe*. No one but me."

Okay, game over. My Gaelic was minimal at best, but I knew what he'd just called me. *My heart.* There might be someone in the universe with the willpower to resist Lachlan Brodie after that, especially when his eyes crinkled at the corners with his soft smile, but that someone was not me.

"The heat's already on down below?"

"Aye."

"There's towels?"

"On the locker by the transom, ready and waiting."

"Coffee?"

"In the galley."

"The berth's got plenty of blankets?"

"Oh, aye." He waggled his eyebrows. "But you won't be needing those, not with me to warm you."

I blinked, suddenly dizzy as my blood rushed south. "Let's go."

He chuckled again as he slipped his arms into the skin— which isn't as creepy as it sounds. His seal skin looks more like a super-deluxe wetsuit than a deboned seal. "Trust me, *mo cridhe*, you can't be any keener than I am to have you in my bed at last."

If that was the case, then I didn't know why we had to endure virtual cryo-immersion first, but...*mo cridhe*? Nope. No way could I turn him down now.

I shrugged out of my jacket. *Brrrr.* "So how does this work, exactly?"

"I'll go in first and shift. Then you slip over the transom, easy as you please, and get on my back."

The transom was at least close to the water, so I didn't have to negotiate a ladder. The sea wasn't especially rough today—it was cloudy, normal for Oregon at this time of year, but not stormy—but it was still the ocean, so, you know, not exactly motionless. "On your back?" At least my front would be warm. Ish.

"Aye. Put your arms around my neck." His gaze was hot, intent, and I'd never heard Lachlan *breathless* before. "And we'll swim. Together."

"Okay." I tried to put a little more confidence into my voice. "Right. Let's do this."

He kissed me, soft and slow. "Thank you, *mo cridhe*. You have made me the happiest of men."

The seal fur didn't give me anything to grab onto, so I laced my fingers behind his neck. "You're *sure* we can't skip the naked swim and go straight to bed?"

"I'm sure." He kissed me again, far too quickly for my liking, and strode across the deck and down the starboard stairs to the low transom. He slipped into the water without a splash, and between one blink and the next...well, he was a seal, gazing up at me as he bobbed gently in the waves.

"The things I do for love," I muttered.

Dear Reader,

Thank you so much for reading *The Lady Under the Lake*, the third book in my Quest Investigations mystery series! If you're curious about Matt's backstory, you might want to check out his debut on the Mythmatched stage in *Single White Incubus*, the first in the Supernatural Selection trilogy about a paranormal matchmaking agency, or his later appearance (along with Jordan's introduction) in *Howling on Hold*. If you'd like to go all the way back to the Mythmatched beginnings, the story world dawned with *Cutie and the Beast*, a paranormal rom-com where a cursed fae warrior turned psychologist clashes with his determined temporary office manager. As you might expect, hijinks ensue!

You can see all my books on my website, https://ejrussell.com, or on my Amazon author page here: https://www.amazon.com/author/ej_russell. Most are also available at Apple, Kobo, and Barnes and Noble.

Would you like exclusive content and ARC giveaways, not to mention gratuitous dance videos? Then I'd love for you to join me in Reality Optional, my Facebook fan group (https://facebook.com/groups/reality.optional). My newsletter is the place to get the latest dish on new releases, sales, and more. I promise I only send one out when I've got...well...news. You can subscribe here: https://ejrussell.com/newsletter.

All my best,
—E

ALSO BY
E.J. RUSSELL

Paranormal Romance
Mythmatched Universe
Fae Out of Water Trilogy
Cutie and the Beast
The Druid Next Door
Bad Boy's Bard

Supernatural Selection Trilogy
Single White Incubus
Vampire With Benefits
Demon on the Down-Low

Other Mythmatched Romances
Howling on Hold
Possession in Session
Witch Under Wraps
Cursed is the Worst

Quest Investigations Mysteries
Five Dead Herrings
The Hound of the Burgervilles
The Lady Under the Lake
Death on Denial

Art Medium Series
The Artist's Touch
Tested in Fire

Art Medium: The Complete Collection (omnibus edition)

Legend Tripping Series
Stumptown Spirits
Wolf's Clothing

Enchanted Occasions Series
Nudging Fate
Devouring Flame

Royal Powers Series (shared world)
Duking It Out

Monster Till Midnight

Historical Romance
Silent Sin

Contemporary Romance
The Thomas Flair
Mystic Man
For a Good Time, Call… (A Bluewater Bay novel, with Anne
Tenino)

Holiday Shorts (separately)
The Probability of Mistletoe
An Everyday Hero
A Swants Soiree
or all three together in
Christmas Kisses

Geeklandia Series
The Boyfriend Algorithm (M/F)
Clickbait

E.J. Russell–grace, mother of three, recovering actor–writes romance in a rainbow of flavors. Count on high snark, low angst and happy endings.

Reality? Eh, not so much.

She's married to Curmudgeonly Husband, a man who cares even less about sports than she does. Luckily, C.H. also loves to cook, or all three of their children (Lovely Daughter and Darling Sons A and B) would have survived on nothing but Cheerios, beef jerky, and Satsuma mandarins (the extent of E.J.'s culinary skill set).

E.J. lives in rural Oregon, enjoys visits from her wonderful adult children, and indulges in good books, red wine, and the occasional hyperbole.

News & Social Media:
Website: https://ejrussell.com
Newsletter: https://ejrussell.com/newsletter
Facebook Reader Group: https://www.facebook.com/groups/reality.optional
Amazon: https://amazon.com/author/ej_russell
BookBub: https://www.bookbub.com/authors/e-j-russell
Facebook: https://facebook.com/E.J.Russell.author
Twitter: @EJ_Russell

ACKNOWLEDGEMENTS

Many thanks to my awesome beta readers—Kelly Jensen, Lisa Leoni-Kinley, and lyric apted—for suggestions, advice, and encouragement; to Meg DesCamp, Queen of Puns, for editing magic; to L.C. Chase for the adorable cover; to my family for endless support; and of course to you, my readers, for accompanying me on this wild journey.

Without all of you, I wouldn't be able to continue to do what I love.